MW01534521

SHADES OF PINK

SCOTTIE KAYE

ELUSIVE PRESS
IT'S IN THE CHASE

ISBN: 978-1-952214-24-0 (Kindle eBook)

ISBN: 978-1-95-221426-4 (Softcover)

Library of Congress Control Number: TBD

This book is a work of fiction. Names, characters, places and events are products of the author's imagination, and any resemblances to actual events or places or persons, living or dead, is entirely coincidental.

Front cover design by Paladin Book Design.

Links may be affiliate links.

Printed by Kindle Direct Publishing. Published in Westland, MI, USA.

First printing edition 2020.

www.elusivepressbooks.com

www.scottiekaye.com

ALSO BY SCOTTIE KAYE

The Sleeping Lotus Series

The Rose Contract

The Marigold Room

The Morning Agent

The Wolfsbane Cipher

The Foxglove Shift

The Orchid War

The Sleeping Lotus

The World of Sense Collection

First of Her Kind

Lady of Chains

Bring Me Down

The Heart of Touch

Shades of Pink

To Emma, my best example of "great minds think alike."

ONE

THE MANY SHADES OF PINK

Triggers: MF, age difference, prostitution.
Companion Book: The Heart of Touch.
Spoilers: None.

R ock Barren's inn was a junk-hole of a place, and it didn't see many beautiful women. The ones it *did* see were often bought by the hour.

At first, he thought she was no different.

The woman arrived mid-week and ordered an ale, before sitting alone at the bar. It was an early part of the night, before the patrons got drunk. Within twenty minutes, she had a customer.

A shame, Rock thought, as she led the man through a side door, presumably to find privacy in the alley beyond it. This made him nervous, as so many things did now. Ever since his wife....

The thought sharpened to a point, and he shut it out. The grief was a year old, but still vicious.

Despite his worries, the woman returned only five minutes

later, to order yet another ale. He brought it to her without saying anything. She sipped the beer and stared at the wall of liquors behind him. Not wanting to see his judgment, no doubt.

Before an hour had passed—before the sun was even down —a man stepped up beside her. Rock listened without appearing to listen, cleaning a glass at the bussing station of the bar.

"Hey, gorgeous. What brings you to Soma?" the man asked, leaning casually onto the bar. Rock knew him as a rich merchant's son who visited the Sleeping Lotus when he wanted to "live low."

The woman turned to him and smiled with such brilliance that even Rock paused in cleaning his glass. She was Gustatory, her skin ebony-black, a foreigner with strange hazel eyes. When she smiled, her beauty staggered his heartbeat. It was daunting, how perfect she was.

She angled herself toward the man in a challenging way, her arms pushing her breasts up and emphasizing their size. Rock tore his eyes off her as she gave her response.

"A thousand marks," she said, "and I'll tell you."

Rock nearly whistled. She'd pegged her target right. Despite the man's rough dress, she knew he was a noble. She must have charged the last man much less.

"That's a bit on the expensive side," the noble said.

She shrugged. "What can I say? I'm expensive."

If that were true, Rock thought, *then why'd you order cheap ale?* A foreign wine seemed much more her style.

"Seven-hundred-and-fifty," the man countered.

The woman drained her ale. "Nine hundred," she said.

This time, she was out back for longer.

It was hard not to watch her after that, given he'd take any diversion that he could get. Being mid-week, it was a slow night as well, and Rock had hired extra servers to take the weight off him. He should let them go soon, but it was still hard to function. He couldn't stop thinking about what he had lost.

When the woman returned, still unrumpled, from her third client that night, he poured her an ale and said, "On the house."

She looked up at him with hazel eyes that had so many colors it was like looking at paint spatter on canvas. She sipped the beer and said, "Why thank you, handsome."

"My name's Rock," he said, "not Handsome. You don't have to do that with me."

She pouted at him with full midnight lips. "Oh, but what if I want to?"

Rock held up his ring finger. The ring was still there. She didn't have to know that his wife was dead.

"Shame," she said, sipping the ale again, her voice still lilting with subtle flirtation. Despite himself, her interest gave him flutters. He tried to think of something to say.

He crossed his arms on the bar top and settled onto them. "What *does* bring you here, anyway? Don't get many Gusta from here."

"Just passing through," she replied.

"Where do you hail from?" he asked.

Her eyes flickered, her mouth parting. She wasn't used to this question.

She smiled again. "The capital. Taste."

"I got a friend there," he said. "Owns the big inn, the Blue Duck. You ever been?"

She shrugged with one shoulder. "Once or twice. Decent ale."

He pursed his lips, backed off, and left her. There was no such place as the Blue Duck.

THE NEXT DAY, another stunning woman sat at his bar, wearing a dress that must have cost half a fortune. He wondered if there were some sort of beauty contest in town. He knew of a dress shop that sometimes hired models.

"What'll you have," he asked her.

"Ale," she replied.

Ale again? For a beautiful woman?

"I thought Auditory women liked white wine," he commented, pouring the beer until it foamed over the edge. This woman was pale, with hair fairy-golden, and violet eyes with all the vibrancy drained out of them.

"I like to try the local fare," she replied, taking the beer with deft fingers. He noticed then that she did not wear a nullband. Strange, he thought, for a woman with money.

"Can I ask your name?" he said.

Her eyes rose to his as she took a sip. The motion struck him as very familiar.

"You can have whatever you want, for two hundred marks," she said softly. He chose to respond with a laugh.

"Miss," he said, "I've got two kids in boarding school. I haven't got three marks to spare." He'd have more, of course, if he let the extra servers go, but he didn't tell her that.

He expected a response like "too bad" from the woman, but instead she looked away. "You have children?" she asked after a moment.

"Yeah, two. Cliff and Firra. Cliff's eight and Firra's five. A whole heap of trouble, the both of them."

"Sounds like you miss them," she said softly.

"Like you wouldn't believe. But my wife—"

He stopped himself as the knife stabbed up through his stomach. The woman noticed, her eyebrows rising. "Are you all right?" she asked.

His throat was dry. "Yes." He moved away.

That night, he dreamed of violet eyes.

THE NEXT DAY, now a weekend, a third woman arrived. She was Olfactory, copper-skinned, with eyes of purest gold, and curls that drew the eye into her prominent cleavage. Like the other women, she wore fine clothing, and her skin was so unblemished that it seemed to shine. She sat at a table, not the bar, but Rock served her anyway. He'd fired one of his servers hat very morning.

"This beer is free," he said, holding it over her, "if you can tell me what's going on. You're the third pretty girl in my bar this week. Is there a brothel that shut down somewhere, or something?"

She hesitated in a way he found familiar. Lips parted, eyes seeming to quiver. The déjà vu passed as she smiled. "How did you know?"

He placed the beer in the center of the table.

It was a large table, meant to hold eight patrons at once, so she had to stretch out her arm to take the ale. When she did, he saw that her wrist was bare. No null-band. Again.

He sat next to her, quickly and suddenly. She stopped going for the beer and turned.

"I've heard of your kind," he whispered, low enough that no one else could hear.

She blanched, making it even more obvious. "I don't know what you mean."

"You're a skinchanger," he said. "And this is the third time you've been here."

Her hands sank into her lap, and she glanced around the room. "What do you want?" she whispered.

It was true then. Amazing. To think he'd meet such a rare mage, one who could change her—or *his*—form at will.

"I want you to keep coming back," he said, "until I can afford you. And I want your name."

She swallowed. "Salihah. It's Salihah."

He chuckled. "So you really are Gustatory. Was that your real body, the first night you came?"

Her lips pressed tight together. They were such kissable lips. Of course a woman so perfect could not be real.

Rock reached out for the ale and slid it toward her. "My wife died a year ago, Miss Salihah," he said. "I just want to see her one last time. I'll pay what you ask, and I'll keep your secret. You can operate in my inn as long as you like."

ROCK FIRED ALL his extra servers; none of them had been very good anyway. By the time a week passed, he'd saved enough marks to buy her. But it took him several more days just to work up the courage.

And each day, he talked with her. He asked nothing personal. He told her about his dead wife, then his kids. She seemed particularly curious about his children, which seemed rather odd for a courtesan. But he was always happy to answer whatever she asked.

"Good morning, Rock," she said, on the tenth day they had known each other. She arrived even before he was technically open.

"You ever consider resting?" he asked as she sat down at the bar. The earlier she showed up, the more clients she could seduce. "You must have a fortune by this time."

Her smile was subdued. She wore Soma skin this time, a

milky brown with cool tones, and her eyes were a riveting bluish green.

"I wish I did," she said, "but I'm saving for something. And I'm running out of time. I can't stop."

"How much do you need?" he asked, curious.

"Eighteen-thousand-five," she replied.

The number hit him hard. He'd heard it once before. The specificity of it was hard to miss. He scoured the shadows of his inn, and when he was sure no one was there, he put his hand on hers and drew her eyes to his own.

"Salihah," he said seriously, "you're being cheated. You'd be better off visiting Audit."

She paled and said, "I'm sorry?"

"That's the number the Blood apothecary gave you, am I right?" He really hated that man.

Her hand tensed beneath his. "How can you possibly know that?"

"Because we went to him once. My wife and I."

Her eyes were wet now. Getting wetter. "But—you have children," she breathed.

"We almost didn't have Firra," he explained. "She was the child of a rape. I inquired, and I would have paid it, but my wife didn't want to, and we raised Firra as mine. Later I met a doctor out of Audit, and he said that there, the operation is free."

Her eyes darted now, as if she were thinking of running. He squeezed her hand and straightened.

"You're taking a room today," he said, "and you're getting a rest. I'm sure you have a lot to think about, and I want you to have the space to think it."

Her voice rose in pitch. "But there's nothing to think about." She stood off the bar chair. "I need to go to Audit. I can hire a carriage now. And when it's over, I'll have money left—"

"Just rest," he said, "just one day and one night. The room's on the house. Trust me, you need it."

She rounded on him, her skimpy dress swaying. "You don't think I should do it," she said.

He thought of Firra, his firecracker and his darling. And he also thought of his wife, of the long days of her pregnancy, where she stared at a blank wall and did nothing at all.

"Salihah," he said, "if I haven't judged you for selling yourself five times a night, do you really think I'd judge you for this?"

IN THE WITCHING hours of the next morning, Rock lay down, exhausted. Without the extra servers, the work was twice as hard. He was having trouble getting used to it, but it was still a relief. He felt alive for the first time in a year.

He rolled over in his bed and touched the painting on the wall, its thick brush strokes worn from how often he stroked it. It was an image of his family he'd ordered when Firra had turned two, when things were better, when his wife used to smile. He traced that smile now, feeling a warmth in his chest. He'd loved her more than anything.

And now she was gone.

A knock sounded at his door, and he frowned and stood up. The door to his apartments was clearly marked in the hallway; after all, he was the caretaker for his inn. Any of his patrons could call for his help any time, so he stepped up to his door and peered out.

A young woman stood there, one he didn't recognize. She looked like a carriage had run her over, then backed up to run her over again. Under her eyes, her dark skin was flat black, darkened by circles that proved she rarely got sleep. Her pink dress hung off her frame like bloody linen, and her eyes were night-black from her magic.

But the dress was familiar, and her cheeks were wet. "Salihah," he realized. "Is that you?"

"Can I come in?" she asked softly.

He was too startled to do anything but swing his door open. He closed it behind her before he thought better of it. She barely looked twenty years old.

"Is this—is that you?" he asked. She was staring at his family portrait. "Your—your true form, I mean."

"She was lovely," Salihah said, not answering his question, and that was when she started to change. His stomach turned as her skin sank into her, melting like wax. Colors mixed, muscles bunched, and hair lengthened. It made him so nauseous that he had to sit down at his desk, and when his wife turned and looked at him, he pressed a fist to his gut.

"No," he said. He looked away. This woman was not his wife.

"I'm leaving tomorrow," she said, "and I just want to thank you. Please, let me do this for you."

He scrunched his eyes closed, as tight as they could go. He'd thought he had wanted this, but he couldn't bear it. His wife was dead, and this was not her. This was just a young woman—far, far too young. A woman who had been through enough.

"Please," he said, "change back."

A pause. "Which of me would you like?"

It took him a second to process the question. "None of them. Just the real you."

He heard her swallow. Moments passed. Her hand curled around the one he had shoved into his stomach.

"Rock," she said, and he opened his eyes to find her kneeling. Her other hand closed on his thigh. "I want to do this. Let me do it—for me. It helps me clear my head."

She looked so frail, and so very tired, her bushy hair tangled, her hazel eyes dim. All the resounding beauty had gone out of her. This was who she really was.

"You're too young," he said, but his body was already responding. A woman hadn't touched his leg since months before his wife passed. She noticed, too, and her palm slid off his fist, over his navel, down to his groin.

"I'm of age," she said, her finger trailing up and down. "And I'm no wilting flower. I know what I'm doing."

"That's not—it wouldn't be—"

"Right? I'll decide that." She laid both hands flat and pushed them up toward his belt. He sat stock-still as she unclipped the buckle, pulling it inch-by-inch out of its loops.

He didn't realize until that moment how badly he wanted. Not Salihah herself, but anyone whatsoever. He hadn't been touched in so very long.

"I didn't need this from you," he whispered. It was his last defense.

Her fingers folded into his breeches, and she found his hot flesh.

He leaned forward, breathing hard, his hands gripping the chair seat as her fingertips caressed his bare skin. A stronger man could deny her, but he'd forgotten why he should. All he could think about was the agony of his want.

Tentatively she pulled his clothes off, exposing his bare thighs, her fingers roving up his shaft, then around it, then down. He watched her do it, a massage without pressure, her skin the color of night against his. The candle on his bedside table guttered as if his breaths could reach it even from here.

For a long time she touched him, swaying him this way and that. Her eyes grew brighter at each angle she surveyed him.

He could see down her dress, to her flatter chest, her nipples obvious in the shadows of her neckline. Her touches turned firm, her hand fisted and pulsed, until his hips were moving back and forth with her motion.

Rock hung his head back, groaning low in his throat. He had forgotten what this sort of thing felt like. When he and his wife had been young, before Firra's horrid conception, they used to worship each other just like this. Fingertips over flesh, curious and exploratory, then a slowly pumping fist, then raking strokes and heavy breaths borne of effort.

That's what it was now, her hand rough and fast, the eye of his penis leaping toward him as skin bunched around it. Rock gripped her by the back of her scalp, but he didn't push down. He only did it to touch her, to connect with her somehow. Her intensity was slowly pulling him off the chair.

A quiver shook up his shaft, his balls tensing—no, squeezing. She'd touched them with a hand, pinching the skin between them. While he was distracted by this, her mouth came down.

He exhaled a half-moan of surprise as warm wet sucked around him, the pressure of swallowing, the whisper of teeth. She pulled him into her throat, where her muscles closed from her swallow. Her tongue darted back-and-forth along the underside of his penis, where the flesh was the most tender, at the thick vein where his semen had gathered.

Then his cock jumped, like a warning, and he knew how close he was. He took Salihah by the shoulders and shoved her back. Her heat left him with a pop, and he angled forward off the chair, nudging her backward until she lay flat.

Her legs raised around him as he settled between them, her eyes closed, and she said his name. She was a decade younger than him, at least, but he could read her by now. Her desire was real, and he felt honored to be wanted, like a long-forgotten bottle of liquor enjoyed all the same.

"Oh, Salihah," he said, and she moaned in response—just a quick sound, before he kissed it out of her. Their tongues met for a moment, and he tasted his own sweat, playing with the same tongue she'd been using to please him.

"Please," she whimpered as he broke the kiss, trailing the tip of his nose down her lips before digging into her neck. He kissed her higher each time, until his nose met her hair, where he inhaled the lemon-lye scent of his own homemade soap.

Salihah arched her hips into him, his bare penis nudging the gauzy pink of her skirts. In response, he tugged up the ruffles until he could lay a palm on her leg, then he rode the skirt up to her hips, ventured over to her heat, and made her gasp as his fingertips flicked.

Then years of need shuddered out of him, and he yanked her underthings aside. He entered her with a jagged groan. When he was quiet again, she sighed into the curve of his ear; he felt a pendulous energy swing through him, and he thrust again, gripping the bottom of her thigh and pushing into her, until the wet of her vagina met the base of his penis.

He repeated the motion, again and again; there was no room inside him to count how many times. Soon they were bent together in a strange broken way, her loose dress exposing one breast. He kissed her bare nipple, sucking down as he thrust. Her head hung back, and he felt her breaths in her stomach, felt new tension in her vagina as she made her body clamp down. It was a trick he'd never felt, not ever. He almost came, and it made him remember himself.

He needed to make her come first.

Rock pulled out of her and ducked down, his mouth on her fast. He licked her as her legs closed on his head. Salihah moaned as he fondled her lips with his own, as his tongue dipped and circled, searching for her pleasure.

He found it, long, much longer than his wife's and so easy to tickle with the front edge of his teeth. The heel of his hand rammed the floor, and his fingers sank into her, three of them tugging at her while his mouth did its work.

"Holy shit," she swore, which made him groan against her flesh. A woman who'd been with dozens of men, and he, Rock Barren, could please her.

Her legs shook around him, and he rocked her with his mouth, sucking on her to a dangerous rhythm. Her hair tickled his nose and her folds grew slick. His erection rubbed the floor, and he might come just from that. If she didn't come soon, he couldn't get back inside her—

He used his last finger then, and did something his wife had always liked. Salihah arched her back as he explored her from behind.

Then pulse, then pulse, then rub, then suck. He pinched her clitoris with his lips, soft flesh to soft, and she shuddered intensely, and he let her go.

Salihah was so small beneath him as he thrust into her one last time, her vagina clenching with each wave of her pleasure. He wrapped his arms around her, cradling her, his hand on the back of her head, his hips doing the work—until they couldn't.

His chest made a ragged beat against hers as his walls broke and he poured himself into her. He thrust again, groaning, and then settled.

Reality returned, angry and slow.

"Salihah, I—" he said into her hair. He couldn't bear to pull out of her. "I didn't think...."

He should have used protection. Should have come on her stomach. This wasn't respectful. What if she hadn't been pregnant?

"Shh," she said, "don't worry. This is only the second time I haven't used protection."

She thought he was worried about disease, and damn if he should have been. Her warm skin grew cooler beneath him, and he extracted himself from their tangle and sat up. She raised herself up on her arms beside him.

"Rock? Are you all right?"

He ran one hand along the back of his neck, covering his privates with the other. He felt suddenly old and predatory before this small, haggard girl. He noticed for the first time that her stomach was rounded.

Heat rampaged up his neck. *I shouldn't have done this.*

Salihah smiled at his blush, and raised herself up. To his surprise, she settled onto his lap, spreading her legs until their tired skin met.

"You know," she said, "for only going missionary, that's the best sex I think I've ever had."

Considering her age, this statement troubled him. She'd had too many lovers to be this young.

"Relax, Rock. I meant what I said. I needed this. Someone who wasn't paying."

He swallowed, but couldn't stop himself from touching her hair, from running the backs of his fingers across the downy puffs. He tried to take her in, from her forehead to her chin, from her dark circles to her candlelit eyes.

"You're beautiful," he said, waiting for guilt to strike him. Waiting to think of his wife.

"That's nice of you to say," she replied, "but I know better. Pretty ladies don't have so many pimples."

He chuckled at that. He could see, perhaps, where she got the idea she was ugly. Her chest was flat, her waist too thin. But he'd hold it all again if she let him. And she'd fill out nice if she just learned to eat.

"My wife was small too," he said. "Maybe I just like small women."

She frowned in concern, but before she could ask, he said, "Don't worry. I'm fine. It's been some times since she passed... I think I needed this too."

They sat in silence for a time, their foreheads together. It was a peaceful feeling, like making a big decision.

"I'm not going to Audit," she said finally. "I'm going to Caress to start a business instead."

He held her arms as he looked up at her. "Caress? Why there?" It was a large town to the north of this one.

"The brothels there are terrible," she said. "Poor percentages for the girls, and stingy madams. The town could use a new place, something nicer. Every town needs a luxury brothel."

Rock couldn't help the frown spreading across his face. "Are you sure you want to do that?" he asked her. "You could do anything you want with that money."

She giggled. "But I like doing this." Her flesh dipped back down to brush against him, and she leaned forward into his ear. "What do you think I should call it? It as to be intriguing. Something that makes you think of sex, but also something refined."

He recalled inventing the Blue Duck inn out of thin air. Perhaps he could come up with something convincing again. But this time he considered for longer, toying with her pink dress as he did. Pink was a good word; it was sexual. But what word spoke of refinement and mystery? Of an anonymous, rich, and beautiful woman waiting to be seduced in a bar?

"The Pink Lady," he said. "Call it the Pink Lady."

And, nine months later, she did.

TWO

ON THE MOSS

TRIGGERS: MMF, FIRST TIME.
COMPANION BOOKS: THE ORCHID WAR, THE SLEEPING
LOTUS.
SPOILERS: SLIGHT.

I t wasn't my fault that men made more sense. Least, that's
what I always told Mags and Li: "Not my fault I like male
company more than I like your sorry asses."

Of course, Anna was the exception. I always told her so.

But once I realized that boys had stopped hanging out with
me over dead squirrels and stick fights, I figured it was about
time to get this virginity thing out of my hair. By that point,
Anna was gone, and Li had taken up most of Anna's patience.
She gave me the rundown on how to please myself. I learned in
about half a week.

"You get there in *how long?*" Mags asked me, once we were
all sitting in our club hut and discussing it. Turns out I was the
last one to the game, at least when it came to getting off.

"Dunno. Couple minutes?" I said.

Mags shook her head, staring out through the half-cocked window, which was more like four sticks tied with twine than an actual opening.

"Takes me ages," she said. "Always has."

Gods, how long has she been doing this? I'm way behind the times.

"Could be cuz she's new at it," Li offered.

Maggie shook her head. "No. Always taken me that long." She eyed me. "Who you thinkin' of, when you do it?"

I shrugged. "Tirim and Merrik, I guess," I said. Tirim could pass as a tree if he stayed still enough, and for some reason, I always liked that. Merrik was just deadly handsome but he was too goofy to get me all the way.

"Well, you have to pick one, if you're gonna have sex," Maggie said.

I crossed my arms. "Who says?"

She rolled her eyes and made a *cuh* sound at the back of her throat. "Well, cuz you can't have two at once!" she snapped.

"Least not for your first time," Li explained. "That's funky stuff. You save it for later."

I laughed. "You ever had two girls at once?"

She blushed, and I kinda wished I was gay. She got cute when she blushed, like stuffed-animal cute. Made me want to hug her and rub my fist on her head, just to make her blush some more.

"Seriously, though, pick one," Maggie said.

"Easy for you to say," I told her. "You been after Cliff since we were six. I've had a new crush every week." I tap my chin. "No. I think I'll do both."

They laughed, then they argued, then they threw up their hands. They'd made the mistake of telling me I couldn't do something. So of course I had to do it.

Still, they had a point. One of the boys *had* to be first. Two of 'em couldn't use the same hole at once. Well, maybe they could, if they wanted. But they wouldn't. I think boys are just weird about that.

"So what do you think?" I told Merrik and Tirim, after I pitched them the plan.

Tirim was frowning in a long sort of way. He did everything a long sort of way; you can't help it when you're that kind of tall.

"The best kisser?" he said, dopily. "And we both gotta be there? Like at the same time?"

I crossed my arms, bad habit. "Yep. My first time's gotta be special, you know. Nothing more special than taking two at once. 'Long as you don't brag about it and make me look like a hoe-ass. You gonna brag and make me look like a hoe-ass?"

Tirim blanched a little. "No, ma'am," he said.

"When?" Merrik asked.

I raised a shoulder, dropped it. "Now?"

We were in the woods, by one of the creeks where we used to strip naked as kids. Back when Anna was still around. But being naked has long since meant more, and Merrik's probably had eyes on me the longest. He stares at my boobs at least once every day.

"All right," he said. He glanced at Tirim. "Like, should I kiss you now, or does he turn around, or wha—"

I get tired of stuff quickly, so I just pulled him into my mouth. I put him up against a tree while he gurgled. Then finally he figured things out, opened his mouth and dove right in. Whoa, didn't think he had it in him. Spun me right around, against a tree, bark and one knobby branch digging in against my spine as his tongue danced. I'd kissed before but he wanted to earn it this time. Cleaning me out. Leaving me dizzy. We knocked teeth a couple of times.

It did magic for me downstairs, the kind I knew I could take care of in maybe thirty seconds. *Excuse me, boys,* I could tell them, and dip out and flex my fingers and come back again. But that was their job today, wasn't it? Mags had told me not to count on it.

"Your turn," I told Tirim, and I actually blushed. There hadn't been much left of my voice.

He looked scared. Merrik backed off, knew better than to counteract my rules, but he was smug. He'd won, of course. Nothing for it but to let poor Tirim trundle through things and earn second place between my legs.

I heard him swallow, his neck higher than my face. Nervous. Hands rubbing his own hips. He towered over me, casting shadow even though it was night, there was just *that* much of him.

"Um," he said, raising a hand. It just sat there a minute, in midair, and he went to take it back and then paused and then stuck it to my cheek. He kissed me the same way, in a stop-and-start, um-maybe-yes-no, but he kissed me eventually and it was soft-like and his hand was still on my cheek.

Tirim got closer and I had been smiling, almost laughing but I wasn't anymore because he was pressing against me. Hand to my cheek, lips seconds from mine, and his body hard on my stomach because he was so tall he didn't fit between my legs perfect. But I felt him there and he kissed me again, his tongue sliding along my lip this time and then dipping past them and parting my teeth.

Oh, gods. It was slow. He picked me up and pressed himself to the proper spot and my body burned and he still kissed me slow like he wanted to taste me. I forgot Merrik was there, I think Merrik even forgot Merrik was there because he didn't complain, he just watched too.

"I want you, Firra," Tirim breathed hot in my ear. He still sounded uncertain but also lost in his uncertainty.

"You got a big brother?" I said, but my voice wasn't there. "Someone to teach you all this?"

"Just a good imagination," he said, which I knew of course, I knew all the boys' brothers and he was an only child; then he was lowering me back to the ground. I couldn't really handle all the intake, then, too much heat and want. I took his hand and led it past my waistband and he groaned a little, a small sound just for me as he touched me. He was clumsy then in all those wet spaces and he only got to the good spot by accident. But he got there and I was already finished.

I remembered where I was again a few seconds later, clinging to him. Merrik watched us pink-faced and embarrassed and I blink and I felt bad. So I pulled Tirim's face down and spoke right up to his ear, "You get to go first." Then I walked to Merrik and took off his pants.

I don't know if they watched each other. They could have. I could imagine Tirim with his hand fishing around in his own trousers as I let Merrik's belt fall around his ankles. I pushed him against a tree the same way he'd pushed me, swam my tongue around his tongue a little and then got right on my knees and let Merrik be first at *something*, at least.

Don't know what I expected. It was interesting. I waited too long to do this and now I got to feel sloppy and new when I should know what I'm doing. Merrik seemed to know, cuz he buried his head in my hair and I thought he'd push me but it actually took him a while to start doing that. First I got to map the shape of him. Soft and hot and salty with this weird smell, like sweat but it makes you think of wet corn husks or, you know, mold, but the forest kind of mold, the good kind, the way the woods get thick with it when the air is too hot—

It made me gag and I liked it. I was embarrassed when I made noise, hacking down on him, can't be very attractive but his knees shook, I could feel them do it because my palms were on the backs of his bare legs. I went faster, the foreign object sliding up and down my tongue and making my cheeks hurt and that's when he pushed my head into him and sped me up.

"Gods, I want to fuck you," he exhaled, forgetting himself completely, I could tell because after that it was a single curse word repeated about six times and then his flesh tightened in my mouth and my vagina went all twisty again as he did what men do and had an orgasm where he wasn't supposed to.

I felt the spasm on my tongue, I made a little surprised noise and learned what happened when men came. It was a helluva lot different than what happened with *women*. He kept holding me tight to him, and when his hand loosened he said "sorry" and I pulled away and spat and did *not* wait at all. I turned to Tirim. He had his hand in his pants after all.

I scowled at him. "You better not—"

He shook his head and reached for me and he pulled me to my knees as he sank to his, one of his hands still working.

"Oh, you've definitely done this before," I told him as he pulled my belt through its buckle with one hand.

"No," he said, fingers rimming my prickling flesh as he got a grip on my own boy-trousers and pulled. "Just thought about it a lot," he admitted, exposing me. I tried to close my legs because suddenly, ridiculously and completely, I did *not* want him to see.

He slapped my leg away and leaned forward, on both his palms now. I thought he'd get right into town down there, but he surprised the five hells on me by putting his head between my legs.

So *this* is what it's like to be a woman.

I marveled in that adulthood as the urges built. I'd learn later that he was clumsy and overeager but I had an orgasm anyway, the kind that made Maggie so jealous, too fast and too easy. But it felt short, truncated, frustrating as my shuddering legs closed on his face and he pushed them back and rose above me and did it.

I remember my mouth being open several seconds before I asked, "Is it in?"

Later I'd apologize. What a stupid thing to say! It's basically the same thing as "Five gods, are you *small!*"

But he wasn't small, and I figured that out as he started to move. I was just wet and expecting pain and instead I was smooth and slick and my back was arched as he made brand-new sensations against all those flickering muscles. We breathed a lot. My shirt was still on but he got a hand under it and when his fingers closed on my boob he closed his eyes and arched his head down and started to breath loud with each time he swept forward into me. My hips rolled as I learned how to meet him, and my head fell back off a little dip in the ground so my throat felt white in the moonlight.

He said my name; I never said his. He must have loved me; I would think that later. He punched the earth by my head and he thrust his hardest at the moment he broke.

Tirim kissed my neck when he dipped out of me, leaving empty places and moisture. I could feel the glaze in my own eyes as I rolled my head. Surely Merrik would have left, unable to bear the jealousy of going second.

He hadn't. And Merrik went second.

Sloppy, fast, smaller but wilder. He made me twist into new shapes as we made a track across the dirt, until my hands found a root and I gripped it hard as the *low* front of him pressed hard against the *low* front of me, and I thought it would happen a third time, the orgasm, oh wouldn't Maggie be jealous.

"You like that, you like that don't you," he murmured clumsily into my hair, and it wasn't until he said it that I realized I'd been making noise, all kinds of noise all along, even with Tirim, great creative cries and sobs and begs. I was, I discovered then, a *loud* one, the sort of lover that people pretend to be when they're trying to make their friends blush. Merrik rode me partway up the trunk of a tree before he claimed me, splashing that hot stuff inside me and bending away to look down at the place where we met as if seeing it made it a thousand times better.

I let him shiver a few times and we breathed together. Tirim sat against a tree a ways back, looking up at the sky. I pushed Merrik away and closed my legs and drew up my trousers and moved to Tirim. I put my head in his lap to sleep, pausing only long enough to dig into my pocket for the handful of orchid leaves Maggie had given me. *You only need one,* she said, but I was dazed and actually a little worried. Two boys meant a lot more seed, right? So I ate them all.

I thought he'd leave, but Merrik surprised me again, scooting closer. I felt Tirim tense and I looked at both of those young men as they avoided looking at each other. Surely we'd all spring apart and this would be an embarrassing memory for the rest of our days.

We fell asleep together instead, looking up through the leaves at the stars. The night was ours, all three of us, a secret and a trend just beginning. It would take years for me to realize I loved them both the same (even though only Tirim deserved it), and another year after that before I realized that I didn't love either one of them *enough.* But all that was the future, and for now, we had the stars and the dirt and the moss, where we used to have mud pies and dead squirrels and stick fights.

I smiled in my place at the center of them. Tomorrow I'd tell Maggie *I told you so.*

THREE

WHAT HE DESERVES

Triggers: MF, adultery, BDSM.
Companion Books: Various.
Spoilers: None.

There was nothing quite so monstrously boring as an Auditory argument, especially when there was a marriage in the mix. Arani tolerated it as only a true princess could; by sitting at the back of the room full of men, while one of her favorite maids did her nails.

"The entire concept of a dowry is absurd!" shouted her father, King Sudheno. "You'll receive an entire country as an ally. Open trade routes and lands! And if either of us should ask for money, it should be us!"

"No dowry, and we have no deal," said the Somatosensory diplomat, an old man who gave Arani the creeps. "Soma is one of the largest nations. King Rastus could easily marry into any one of the smaller nations. What can you offer that they cannot?"

"This isn't an auction!" her father boomed. Arani yawned,

glanced without interest at her likely future husband, Rastus. Handsome enough, but not exciting; he would occasional dip his head at her, but no more; she'd gotten more attention from footmen than from him.

She realized then that her maid had stopped painting her nails, and was now holding Arani's left hand limply while staring off into a corner of the conference room. Frowning, Arani followed her gaze to a man standing in the shadows where two paneled walls met. His eyes flicked from the maid, and Arani caught him partway through licking his lips; his wet tongue hung there, glistening in the lamplight. Half of his mouth smiled.

Arani had barely recognized him as the Soma king's brother when he pushed off the wall and boomed—in a voice so authoritative, it made her jump—"Enough of this. She isn't a virgin."

Arani's stomach dropped, so fast it was hard at first to recognize the emotion behind it: indignation. It seemed much the room felt the same way, because nobody spoke. The man—Ragen was his name—strode up to the conference table, turned slightly, and sat right on its surface. He picked at something on his nail and continued,

"In Soma, a woman's flower has value. A deflowered woman is worth a quarter what a virgin is. Some aren't even marriageable at all. And you are suggesting we pay for her hand?" He looked up, and once more he met her eyes. Not her father's, not the councilors', hers. "As far as I've heard it," he went on, "if we subtracted even ten marks for each time this one's been stuck, our entire country would go into debt."

Arani narrowed her eyes and ground her teeth, but said nothing. Her father sputtered his outrage, and someone said something about how many times the Soma king had stuck someone, and if it could all be put on a scale—just ridiculous.

Through it all, Ragen kept watching her.

Arani's maid shivered, herself still captured by Ragen's presence, and hurriedly she set back to work on Arani's nails, her hair, her perfume. Suddenly Arani hated the woman's touch. She hated the frivolity of it all, with this man's leering gaze on her. She was not a trophy to be displayed and argued over, and she most certainly was not a whore. She was a gods-damned princess of Audit, and she could sleep with whomever she pleased.

With that thought at the front of her mind, Arani drew in a great huff and shot to her feet. The room fell silent, thrown by the movement. She glared at Ragen as she opened her mouth.

Her future husband, King Rastus, beat her to it.

Into the sudden silence, he said, "Give these Auditory gentlemen whatever they want. All I want in exchange is my wife."

With that he rose, met her eyes, and smiled at her for the first time. It wasn't the smile of a desperate lover, but the smile of a man who shared the same frustrations. He didn't want to be here either; he didn't want to argue or bemoan. And when his creepy old advisor tried to sway him, Rastus held up a single hand, shook his head, and left.

"You're dismissed," Arani said to her maid once he'd gone. Her maid nodded and scurried away, and Arani's gaze was drawn back to Ragen, the brother. He stood casually, flipping his coat over his arm. With a dirty smile flung her way, he left also, leaving all the advisors to hash out the details.

⬣

IT WAS NEARLY a half hour before Arani was allowed to leave, and all that time she remained standing, her pulse pounding, with nothing to do and nothing to be done to her. She could almost feel her hair fraying, her skin sweating. Why had she sent the maid away? Was she truly so unfamiliar with criticism, that she'd be so incensed by Ragen's jab? Who did he even think he was, anyway? Somatosensory customs had no sway in this country. How many sexual partners had he had?

Her thoughts raced with these meaningless, furious thoughts as she stormed back to her quarters, refusing every offer of a moist towel or a brush of her hair. She demanded to be left alone as she stepped through her sitting room to her chambers.

Then she opened the door—and saw the maid.

The maid was the first thing her eyes glued to, because she was completely naked, shoved against the back of Arani's chaise lounge while a man pulled her hair from behind. The poor woman's dark hair stuck to her neck and forehead, absolutely inundated with sweat. She looked constricted, beaten, forced into place—and if not for the desperate moans crawling out of her throat, Arani might have rung for a guard.

And the man going to town to her was none other than Ragen Wise, brother of the man Arani would marry. He hadn't even taken his clothes off, and he grinned in a rictus of focus as he hammered the woman against him. He had the maid gripped by her hair and her shoulder, and it seemed he was slamming against her behind just as hard as he was pulling her to him. The sheer effort was the first thing that Arani wrapped her head around. The two looked like they'd just run a race.

Then the scene caught up with her, and she opened her mouth, incensed and horrified and utterly bewildered.

"What is the meaning of this?" Arani cried.

Her maid laid a set of wide, surprised eyes on Arani; then gave a very unladylike peep and tried to scramble away from her suitor. Ragen responded by pulling on her hair so hard she cried out, and then he swiveled in place and sat on the lounge, bringing the maid down on top of him.

The moment the woman landed, Ragen bit into her neck and turned his vibrant green eyes on Arani. Both his hands dipped to the woman's vagina and began to massage her. In the space of only a few seconds, the maid forgot that Arani was there.

Arani felt her pale cheeks flushing. Did they expect her to watch this coupling? These were her chambers! Hers!

"You're dismissed, Eseli!" she shouted at her maid. Ragen licked the woman's neck, and she started to breathe in short bursts, sweat dripping off her nose and marking trails down her breasts—

The sight ignited passion in Arani, and she hated it. If she wanted to witness sex, or to have it, she would simply call on a courtesan or two. She had no wish to walk in on such things, much less within her own chambers.

"Stop this!" Arani shouted at them. "And stop looking at me!"

Ragen breathed in Eseli's hair. "When I'm done."

Arani quivered, closing her mouth to keep from sputtering. Her throat tightened with frustration. What was this madness? No one had ever disobeyed her before. Never!

With an exultant cry, her maid orgasmed and collapse backward onto Ragen, who massaged her shoulders and whispered something into her ear. All while he kept watching Arani. Kept smiling at her like some sort of beast.

She should leave, Arani realized. Call for a guard. Yet somehow, she was rooted to the spot as her maid nodded to Ragen and slipped to the floor, pink with pleasure. On her knees, the woman turned to face the crux of Ragen's knees. She brought her head down, and started to suck.

"Ah, there we go," Ragen said. "Now I can relax, and have a nice little chat with my new sister. Come now, Arani. You should sit."

"I'll do no such thing," Arani snapped, still unable to move. She kept her eyes decidedly off the naked woman, but the movement was there. Not that Ragen noticed it. Not that his words gave away what was happening.

"Fine," he said, "you just stand there looking pretty. Those giant tits of yours will only make me come faster."

"You're sick," she said. "Delusional. If your brother—"

"Oh, he doesn't know about this, and he won't, will he?" Ragen said, cocking an eyebrow. The maid pulled close to him, making his abdomen tense, but even the deep-throat didn't affect his expression.

"Is this some sort of game you're playing?" Arani said. "Trying to—to put yourself on display? Test my loyalties?"

"Why?" he asked, cocking an eyebrow. "Are your loyalties being tested? Should I ask her to leave?"

When Arani's only response was to grasp for the nearest handhold to keep herself upright—in this case, the back of a chair—Ragen laughed and spread his arms along the back of the lounge. The maid bobbed, and bobbed, and bobbed.

It was almost like the woman ceased to be human. Ceased to be present, as far as he cared.

"I just want you to know a few things about me, dear sister," Ragen said. "Before your precious vows are exchanged. One: there's nothing Rastus has that I don't have more of. Two: that will soon include you."

With that, he looked down at the woman, and ran a hand lovingly through her hair, and she stopped sucking him off and made a hungry noise in her throat, as if she'd just tasted a heavenly sweetcake. Arani slumped into the chair when she understood what had happened—Ragen had come the very moment he'd felt like it, and his pensive face had not changed at all.

The maid pulled off him, wiping her mouth and standing. She chanced an embarrassed look at Arani before she scurried off to the water closet. Ragen tucked his penis away before Arani could see.

Then he rose like a snake and strode toward her, his regalia clinking with medals. When he reached out to trail his fingers on the flesh between her sleeves and her neck, Arani did not stop him. She was horrified to find that she didn't want to.

"You feel that?" he said, and her skin prickled.

"Feel what?" she said, trying to growl.

Ragen leaned close. "Power," he whispered.

Then he turned and left her alone.

THREE MONTHS PASSED before the wedding. Three months where Ragen never once looked at her. His inattention made her crazy, to the point she had to bring a handkerchief with her everywhere, for the express purpose of shredding it whenever the bull man came near.

And he did come near. Often. Sidling past her in hallways, passing food to her on dinner tables, delivering glasses of wine from the servants to her hands. Always, he treated it like a favor or inconvenience. But always, his fingers brushed her bare flesh.

And the comments he would make. "What a fine bracelet, Arani. Was the miner paid for the ore? I hear Auditory jewelry is excavated by slaves." or "How your hair shines today, Arani. What animal had to die to make your hair oil?" or "What a fine dress, Arani. So very low cut. It truly does set off your best features."

He would say all these things without his green eyes meeting hers. He would lean to the side, and whisper his criticism like an afterthought.

He was snide and boorish. Cocky and voracious. Kings

below, he kept fucking her maids. She had to hire a new one every week, and start sleeping with them herself, just to double-check that they were lesbians.

And when they started to swing toward him too—when she started coming upon orgies—Arani gave up on having a maid altogether. His commentary then shifted to jibes about how disheveled she was. "You truly cannot brush your own hair?"

Every time he did it, she would tear at her handkerchief. Sometimes, at night, she'd scream into her pillow.

Sometimes, she'd do other things.

He touched her. He berated her. But he never tried to take her. He just kept taking from her. He'd have her furniture rearranged, her meals cut back or switched out, her favorite perfume replaced with something else. Her closet filled up with dresses that he loved to criticize.

And she found herself loving every damned second.

"Rage becomes you," he whispered once, after he delivered a glass of juice when she'd ordered the steward bring her red wine. She snatched the wine from his hands and threw it on his tunic. He only laughed and stepped out of the room.

HER WEDDING DAY CAME. He vows were exchanged. People ate and danced and drank. Arani sat still through it all on the throne of a queen. Surrounded by attendants. Looking stunning.

Ragen didn't even glance at her. Ever. Her husband barely did, either, but his gaze wasn't the one that she craved. When Rastus tucked a rosebud into her hair, she barely spared him enough attention to smile.

The day wound down. Her husband pulled her aside.

"You look tired, my love. Go on back to your rooms. I'll stay for us both, and come for you after."

She thanked him with a sigh. He was a good, decent man. She wouldn't mind spreading her legs for him, or having his children, but she didn't have high hopes for an intimate bedroom.

Swarmed by servants, Arani left the great hall, scanning for Ragen beforehand. He was just tipping a glass of wine to some noblewoman's lips when Arani was swept out of the room.

HER ROOMS WERE cold when she arrived, but she sent the servants away. Stripping off her silken dress, she stacked the firewood herself, then bent forward on her knees to light it. Someone had taught her once, sometime; perhaps when she'd been a child. She breathed out as the small flames took hold.

"So you aren't entirely useless," Ragen said, just like she'd known he would. "Would you look at that! You made a flame."

Arani rose to her full height, taking the fire poker with her. She turned to see Ragen leaning against her balcony door frame, letting even more of the cold air whisper in.

She kept herself still, and loose. Let her skin remain cold. She wouldn't flush for him again.

"What are your plans with that poker?" he asked, with his stupid half-grin. He raised an eyebrow. "Maybe I ought to go?"

Arani said nothing. That's all he allowed her to say. If she spoke, then she would just lose the game.

Instead she walked toward him, the poker's tip pointed downward. In nothing but her shift, she closed the gap, until they stood chest-to-chest. Until it seemed the heartbeat she heard wasn't her own.

Ragen raised a hand and pulled on her lower lip with a

thumb. "How glossy your mouth looks. Too much lipstick, perhaps? One would think—"

And she stabbed him in the foot.

The poker didn't go deep, but it did enter flesh. For the first time in her life, she saw him flinch.

Arani leaned closer. "I'm gods-damned gorgeous, and you know it. You've known it since you convinced Rastus to marry me."

His grin slipped off his face. His vibrant eyes dulled. "What makes you think I convinced him?"

"Because you want to outdo him," she said. "You thrive off that want. Everything he has, you have to have more."

His hand found hers, on the poker. "If that were true," he said, his mouth close to hers, "then why wouldn't I simply kill him?"

They both dropped the poker. It clanged to the floor.

"Because you want what he has," Arani whispered to him. "If he's dead, he has nothing at all. For you to be happy, you must have more than your betters. If you were king, who would have more than you?"

It was why he had tormented her. Why he'd made her crave him. Made her want his approval, his body, his gaze. He wanted his brother's property addicted to him. That way, he would always have more of her.

Ragen held her gaze, expressionless, his eyes flat with desire. Their noses touched. Her glossed lips met his.

"Stop fucking my maids," she spoke into his mouth.

His hands closed on the bottom hem of her dress. He raised the fabric clear off her hips.

"That depends, dear sister, on how good you are."

She unbuckled his belt in a single deft movement, jerking him away and then back. "Oh, sweetie. You already know that

I'm good. It's why you've tortured us both these past three months. It's why you picked me to begin with."

He opened his mouth to respond, but she was tired of words. She grabbed his shaft with her cold hands and squeezed him.

She didn't allow him time, after that, for any clever retorts. Didn't give him the chance to take control of the lovemaking. He'd spent three months displaying his power for her. Tonight, she would show him hers.

Arani began with her hands, one palm to his head, her other palm near his base while two of her fingers goaded his balls. Her arms tensed on both sides of her chest, and her breasts swelled up to meet him.

Then she yanked on him, sudden and vicious.

His mouth opened wider. He looked down into her cleavage, unable to see what she was doing. Pulsing her fists, she rammed into his gut. He grunted. She repeated the movements.

It was the meanest, most furious hand job of her life, and she poured three months of horny rage into it. She was pleased to see him grab the balcony door handle for support as she squeezed and released, punched and slammed and pulled.

"You're going to kill me," he said breathlessly.

"Are you so weak?" she replied, spinning her palm on his head, twisting the flesh and making him groan.

Then she went faster, muscles tensing, muscles burning from effort; her pale hair turned mousy with sweat. When his knees started to go, she fell with him. She gripped his wrists and forced them to the stone tiles.

Pinning his arms to the balcony, she went down on him, taking his full penis to the back of her throat. She didn't savor him, or explore him; she only kept up her effort, hawking salty flesh and hot skin.

He was the perfect size to go deep, to tease her throat's

reflexes, without losing control over muscle. She could pound her forehead into his lower stomach, then gag, then continue. Faster, sweatier, angrier—

He twisted when her tongue tried to slither toward his balls, and in an instant, she found herself on her back. Ragen buried one fist in her hair with one hand, ripping off his pants with the other. She reached up and shoved him out of his coat.

Clawing into her scalp, he exposed her throat and bit into it. Arani moaned as the pain of his hunger. He bit his way down her chest, twisting her nipple with his teeth before opening his mouth wide and trying to suck in her full breasts.

"Here," he murmured, nosing her cleavage. "I want to come here. I want to mark you."

"What are you, a fucking dog?" she asked him.

He thrust her hair to the ground, and he rammed inside her.

She cried out from the power, his abdomen undulating against her, his chest rubbing her bare nipples raw. Her shift was a wet tangle between them. With his free hand, he started to toy with her.

Arani lost track of time, cold stone at her back, a frigid wind making her whole body prickle. His fingers played a slow game, pressing hard but barely moving, while the rest of him raged into her with ravenous thrusts—

Finally, finally, a century later, the orgasm started to build. She felt it expand, catching her breath in her chest, tensing her legs against his—

He pulled out. She gasped. His teeth met her vagina. His tongue swirled between them, tugging and gentle, a contrast that took her over the edge.

Ragen didn't waste her pleasure, thrusting back into her, riding the waves of contracting muscle. She felt his erection with more clarity than ever before. She felt the way that he couldn't breathe.

His sweat flicked her cheeks. He started to buck. His eyes were squinted closed, his face a mask of concentration. He's never looked like this with the maids.

She tore her shift, freeing every last inch of flesh. She propped herself up on her elbows even as he gripped her hair. They arched closer together—closer—closer—

With a wet noise he raced out of her and advanced again, slapping both palms to the balcony railing. He rubbed her chest with his penis, still thrusting, still pouring slick sensation through them both. Instants passed before he ejaculated, his semen squirting between her rippling breasts. It pooled in the base of her throat, steaming in the cold wind. When it was over, her brother-in-law slumped against her.

"Numb King feel me," he swore.

"And you thought I wanted your approval," she snorted.

He rolled over. "My brother will come soon—"

"And I should wash."

"Yes."

"You think he won't know?"

Ragen laughed. "He told me not to do this. I promised I wouldn't. I've never broken a promise before."

That he'd do it for this didn't surprise her. A man's wife was the ultimate thing to covet.

"Rastus deserves a better brother," she said, standing up. Pulling her torn dress back over her shoulders.

He groaned to his feet. "He deserves a better wife, too. I'll come see you again, when he leaves."

She didn't argue. It was pointless. They were two wicked people with two wicked addictions, and she would love this man for the rest of her life.

FOUR

TARGET PRACTICE

TRIGGERS: MF, FIRST TIME, AGE DIFFERENCE, PROSTITU-
TION, MENTIONS PAST ABUSE.
COMPANION BOOK: THE FOXGLOVE SHIFT.
SPOILERS: NONE.

Of all the places hidden away in the House of Thorns, Mikail Haze liked the target room the best. It was hidden in the back of the library, behind a secret door disguised as a bookshelf. It was a well-kept secret and a general inside joke, because you had to go down on the librarian to find out about it.

On Kail's first week as a Thorn, he'd discovered the room without meaning to. By the time he'd come of age, he'd had more than enough experience giving head, but he'd known the House to be a different sort of place. Every guard, every servant, every Thorn of the House was used to getting sex in exchange for small favors. If he was going to stand out, he'd have to outmatch his competitors, so he started putting his mouth on anything that he could.

A surprising amount of the guards allowed this, despite most of them being male; the female guards became his best friends immediately. He tried to impress at least one person a day, and he kept up the pace for a week. On day nine, however, he'd come up against a wall: none of the Thorns would let him anywhere near them.

"Give it up, posy boy," a Morning Glory had told him, when he'd tried to rub her leg under a library table. "None of us are going to fall for your shit. You're making our jobs harder, you know."

This had made him smirk. "I'll take that as a compliment."

The Glory closed her book.

"Look," she said, leaning forward, her breasts plopping over the book, "I've been in your shoes, believe me. You're a fish out of water. These women are threatened by you; this is no place for men." She lowered one shoulder and pointed at him intensely. "But you can't go around raising the expectations of our marks. Take my advice, boy. *Get a hobby.*"

Kail crossed his arms. "How am I supposed to attract my Contract if I'm whittling?" he asked. He had hoped some female mark might spread the word, and some lonely noble-woman would call down to have him.

"Don't you have a mentor?"

He shrugged. Orra was keeping an eye out for him. But she was on assignment in the city again. Five gods, he missed the city.

The Glory sighed and pointed to the librarian, a smug little man who wore glasses. "Talk to Morrin. He knows everyone." She went back to her book.

With a shrug, Kail rose. Might as well. He'd even put in extra effort, just to spite her.

He had Morrin sprawled out in a reading nook within minutes, lying on his back on the bench. This nook had a curtain, but Kail didn't draw it. He'd never been shy when he worked.

Morrin's smugness vanished as Kail yanked his trousers down. "I'm not sure about this," the man said.

"You will be," Kail replied. He was used to this from straight men. He gripped the base of Morrin's penis with two fingers, nice and tight, his thumb pressing into the man's testicles as he descended.

"Numb King," the man gasped as Kail went full speed. On men, he rarely bothered with foreplay. Speed and suction and some good solid pumping did the job every time.

He edged into his usual rhythm, a deep-throating maneuver for five loud thrusts and then a pocket in the cheek for ten. He was in the zone within seconds, his sense of smell and taste gone, his thoughts wandering as his mind grew bored. He'd been doing this for so long, it felt like watching clocks tick. He felt it when the second hand quivered.

Morrin slapped a hand to his own mouth and groaned into it, and Kail popped off, letting the man make his mess. He was about to ask his favor when Morrin spoke.

"The bookshelf," the man gasped. "Back left corner. Look for the copy of a book called *The Time Queen*."

This response mystified Kail, but at the same time he was curious. He left Morrin furiously dabbing at his firstcoat.

It turned out that the book in question was woefully miscategorized, a work of fiction in a section full of maps. He tugged on it, and lo and behold, he heard the clicking of a mechanism as the whole bookshelf swung out.

Inside, he discovered a room full of knives on one side, and littered with stuffed targets on the other. The targets looked fresh, so someone must be keeping the place up.

He remembered the Glory's words: *Get a hobby*.

MONTHS PASSED. He grew ever more antsy. If a noblewoman didn't pay for his cherry soon, he'd be leaving this place through a trash chute.

But the target room was always there for him, even when Orra wasn't. He found himself there more and more as the weeks progressed, working his way through the wide variety of knives, getting a feel for how they each acted in the air, how heavily they were able to impact. After a while, he discovered he had a favorite, and he began to train with that blade exclusively.

He named the knife Lili, after his dead mother figure. That way, every time he was able to hit the target in the center, he got to imagine he was stabbing Li's killer. The mystery of her death was a big part of why he still wanted to be a Thorn, even after Li had left him. Thorns knew things, or were *able* to know things.

Someday, he would get his revenge.

On one particularly anxious day—he'd woken up from a nightmare—he went to the target room to find someone else in it. This wasn't rare; it wasn't *that* big of a secret. Plenty of savvy Thorns came to train here, but there was an unspoken rule that they not speak to him, nor each other. It was a place of meditation and violence.

But this woman wasn't a Thorn.

She wore a black skirt and chest wrap, her curly hair tied behind her, bouncing against her back as she threw. An opulent getup lay on the floor behind her—a robe made of sewn metal and coins.

Kail eyed her form as he took up his usual spot, attacking a target shaped like a man. She was lithe and smooth, her skin like bright copper, and she hit the center every time.

"You're not a Thorn," he said, feeling his body respond to her. It always surprised him whenever this happened.

The woman paused mid-throw and turned to face him. She had a long, refined face, curly bangs, golden eyes. Older than him, probably early forties, but she took very good care of herself. In fact, he wasn't sure if he'd ever felt so attracted. She raised an eyebrow when she saw his white sleeve.

"And yet somehow, *you* are," she said, smiling softly. He'd already forgotten what he had just said.

"You don't have an accent," he burst out, suddenly desperate for something to say. She was an Olfactory noble, he was sure of it. He drew closer and held out a hand.

"I'm Kail Haze," he said. "Thorn initiate. First of my kind."

Her smile dipped on one side, going crooked as she shook his hand. Her grip was impressive. It made him think awful things.

"Doctor Illisyne Read," she declared.

His heart rate sped up. "Of the ruling Reads?"

She rolled her eyes. "The very same. Duke Read is my first cousin."

He couldn't believe his luck as she pulled her hand out of his. This woman was incredibly rich.

"What brings you to this place, Doctor Read?" he asked her. "I was under the impression that it was a secret."

"Oh, it is," she replied, bending to pick a knife out of a neat row she had placed by her feet. He watched her throw, his heartbeat skipping as the second blade clanged against the first. They had to be ten paces from the target, but the two blades had landed on the center dot.

"Might I ask how you know of it? Of the Thorns?" Kail said. She eyed him, and he added, "Entirely out of curiosity, I assure you."

Her eyes lingered on him a moment, and then she threw

again. She'd palmed a knife, and he'd never even seen it. The blade joined its fellows in the center of the target.

"How about I tell you the whole story tomorrow," she said, "when we meet back here again, same place, same time?"

Five hells, she was making him hard as a rock. All she had to do was talk.

"Sure thing," he said dumbly.

She nodded, as if to herself. "Good," she said, walking to the discarded dress and picking it up. "How much is the rate for Rose Contracts again?"

His mouth dried up. He told her.

Her golden gaze dipped to his feet and back up again. "Oh, honey. You're worth more than that."

Kail stood there, bewildered, as she threw the dress on over her head. She was a different kind of stunning with all her clothes on.

How would she look with all her clothes off?

"I don't—are you making an offer?" he stammered.

She held a palm out, indicating his crotch. "Looks like someone *else* made the offer first."

AN HOUR LATER, Orra walked in on him masturbating. "I heard a little rumor," she said.

He scowled at her as he pulled his pants back up, standing off the edge of his bed. This wasn't even the first time this had happened. He wished people would just learn to knock.

"What sort of rumor?" he asked, not bothering to be embarrassed.

"The sort that will make you lots of money," she said, crossing her arms. "The queen's head-doctor has put an offer on your Contract."

Kail had to physically fight not to grin. "Can't imagine how that happened," he said.

She poked him in the chest. "You sly dog. Do you know who that woman is?"

"Hot as a fox, that's what she is," he replied.

"Yes. And she's also excommunicated from Olfact. Bet you didn't know *that*."

He frowned. Well, there went the money.

Orra flopped onto his bed, her dreadlocks spidering all around her. She waved a hand at him. "Oh, don't look so disappointed. The woman's self-made. Went to Gusta and studied the human mind, and now she travels all over making rich people feel better." She sighed. "I'm so *jealous*, you have no idea."

Kail could still feel his unspent erection. "What did you call her? A head-doctor? What's that?"

"Just don't tell her your life story. She might diagnose you with something."

He licked his lips. "Oh, that sounds good to me."

KAIL HAD the signed Contract in his hand the next day. He'd arrived an hour early to the target room, just to be safe. He paced the whole time.

I can't believe this. I'm nervous!

He had practically worked himself into a frenzy by the time she arrived. The bookshelf swung inward, she stepped through, then she closed it. Then she grabbed a lonely chair and wedged it under the door.

"A lock," Mikail said. "I like it."

"Don't get to use them much, do you?" she said, walking toward him.

He held up the Contract. "We're all good to g—"

She kissed him before he could finish.

It was a furious kiss, hungry with impatience. Her tongue jammed its way between his teeth like a bolt from a quiver. He dropped the Contract and opened his mouth, his hands already lifting her dress off. She wore the same plain black skirt as before, and he drove his hands under it, gripping her by the bare skin of her rear.

She seized the hair at the base of his cornrows. "You've really never had a woman?" she breathed.

He shook his head. "Never. I'm gay as a king's fool."

"Oh honey," she said, "no you're not."

What came next was not what he expected. The woman pushed him into a wall. She tore the buttons on his firstcoat, then his secondcoat, until finally his chest and stomach lay bare. She kissed him again, her palms on his abdomen. Her lips were soft and just barely sticky, tugging on him, drawing him close.

"I promised you a story," she murmured, looking up at him through long, dreamy eyelashes. "Do you want the long version —" she tugged his belt free "—or the short?"

He had to blink a few times just to see straight. "At the rate you're going, I won't last through either."

She shoved his pants down off his hips.

His penis emerged, more than ready for action. She ran one palm down his stomach, around his base, then cupped his balls as she drew her hand up again. Slowly, painstakingly, she rubbed up the underside of his shaft, curling her fingers over his head.

"I see why they Thorns let you in," she said, squeezing. "A dick like this is a national treasure."

He couldn't breathe. "Wait until you see... my tongue," he managed.

She grinned at him. "Oh, honey. I won't need your tongue."

With that, she put both hands on him and pumped violently. He cried out in surprise, and then she repeated the stroke. He leaned forward, his mouth pressing into her forehead. He was so lost that he didn't even think to kiss her.

"You like that, do you?" she said.

He vaguely admitted that he did.

"Gods. It's like working clay," she said, leaning away to look down. Her mouth was open, curled up in the corners, as if she had just found a gold coin on the ground. "How the hells will I fit that inside of me? I'm going to be sore for days."

Mikail didn't know. He'd never been inside a woman before, only men. Men were tight at the entry point, but warm and soft for the rest. He'd been told a woman could be tight the whole way.

"Let me—for you—" He tried to make the offer, anything to slow her down, to slow *this* down, but the words barely made it out of his mouth. He leaned his head back, his palms and shoulders against the wall. She worked him better than he worked himself.

"Senseless kings, just looking at it makes me wet," she said, laughing manically. She was crazy. She tossed her curly hair back. "So tell me. Why do you think you're gay?"

He was rigid against the wall, as if he were afraid of her. He looked down without moving his head.

"I fuck men," he said poetically.

She cocked her head, her whole body bobbing. "Why do you think that is?"

He closed his eyes. Nothing, literally *nothing* had ever felt this good. How could sex be better?

"Got sold," he said. "As a kid. Guy who bought me only liked little boys."

The stroking slowed for a moment. "Oh honey." She picked

the pace back up, with one hand this time. With the other she cupped his cheek.

"It was your escape," she said. "You probably told yourself you liked it so that it wouldn't hurt. And you said it so much, you believed it."

The words took a few seconds to process. He opened his mouth to argue with her. He'd *always* been gay. That's why his abuse hadn't been all that bad. He'd had it easy, compared to all the others.

But what came out of his mouth wasn't an argument.

Mikail realized that he had just *sobbed.*

Illisyne rubbed a tear off his face. "It's all right, Mikail. Let it out."

He'd never felt so much emotion at one time. Never once in his life. Not when he'd been captured, not the first time they'd broken him. Not even when Li set him free.

And the wildest thing? He had no clue *what* he felt. It was just emotion, raw, a pins-and-needles weight behind his eyes. He sobbed as her hand drove the flesh up his penis, then pushed down again, his balls yearning for mercy.

"Oh shit," he said, his legs turning to water. He was coming. He was *crying,* and he was coming, and he felt like he was on some other planet, like he'd ascended to a place where every-thing was *connected.* His sex, his stomach, his tear ducts, his lips with her breath on them, the masturbatory sound in his ears at once familiar and yet new. He was drawing together and coming apart.

And yet, he couldn't *come.*

He cried out in frustration. The sensations were too much. But his erection seemed stalled, the ejaculation *right there.*

"What are you doing to me?"

"Mmm," she said, slowing, then stopping. "The question is, what are you doing to *me?*"

He could barely see through his own lidded eyes, but his body moved like it was supposed to, reaching out to pull her chest-wrap down and expose her breasts. She had more flesh than the chest-wrap had hinted at, but not quite enough for him to push his dick through the crack. It was only as he thought this that he realized he *wanted* this. He'd never thought about fucking a woman's chest....

She took his hand off her breast and lowered it between her legs. She must have taken off her own skirt, because he could see the trimmed patch of hair, could touch it and cup her, parting the folds with his fingers—

It was the wet that made him lose his mind.

He didn't remember what happened next. He would struggle for years to remember the precise moment he lost his virginity, but it was gone forever, lost to the madness. The next thing he knew, *she* was the one against the wall, her shoulder blades rocking in front of him as he pushed inside her.

He was still crying, and sweating too, his breath pushing his cheeks out. He had a his hands on her ass, which didn't give him the best leverage but *that ass,* and she was helping, pushing back, making sounds he'd never heard in his life, horrible aching moans as he hurt her.

And he was hurting her. Her throat made that clear, even as her pleasure dripped down his cock to his flopping balls. He couldn't even get all the way inside her.

Despite the pain, she was crying out, *Yes.*

She rocked against him, slamming back, and he nearly staggered before doubling his efforts. Gods, it was perfect. Tight the whole way. And the texture—*there was so much texture*—

Illisyne tipped forward, slamming sideways, pressing her cheek and one shoulder to the wall. He moved with her, unwilling to part from the hot grip of her heat.

It wasn't until she groaned and shuddered that he understood what she had been doing. She'd freed a hand to touch herself.

It was so sexy that Kail came too.

They jerked against one another, inside and outside, as he drained his pleasure into her body. Sweat made a thin film between them. He softened but never pulled out.

"Still think... you're gay?" she asked him.

He put his mouth into her hair, breathed in her scent.

"We should go again," he said, "just to be sure."

FIVE

REPEAT AFTER ME

TRIGGERS: MM, BISEXUAL/BICURIOUS, LIGHT
DOMINATION.
COMPANION BOOK: THE ORCHID WAR.
SPOILERS: NONE.

Toben adjusted his belt as he leaned on a horse picket. He often spent time here in the mornings, watching the training field of the war camp. Every day after sunrise, the general would spar here, drawing scores of soldiers with nothing better to do.

Of course, his opponent was the attraction. They'd all seen the general fight hundreds of times, but a noblewoman? Now that was a show. The woman, Raena Barren, was an oddity in the field camp, and her taunts to the general made her a fan favorite. Her smooth hair and strange eyes—and her focused intensity—only added to her quiet mystique.

Like every other man in this camp, Toben had fantasized about her. He liked to think of her taunting him. She'd be naked on his cot, picking her perfect nails, telling him to go on, get it over with. He'd slide in and get lost, her body warmer than she was; he'd come, and she'd sigh him back off her. She would never meet his eyes; he was too unimportant. When it was over, she would say, good enough.

On the other side of the picket, his tentmate, Logan, spat into the dirt. Toben eyed the larger man, who seemed to hate Raena, his brown eyes flat with spite whenever he watched her. But every time Toben came here, Logan tagged along too, like a hooked fish dragged behind on a string.

"She's getting better," Toben commented. As an officer, Logan outranked him, so he often tried to make friends. The man was normally effusive and easy to get along with—but never when he was looking at Raena.

"She's sloppy," Logan countered, even though Raena was as graceful of a beginner as Toben had ever seen. "And what sort of bodyguard does she even have? Leaving her alone in a camp full of soldiers."

The bodyguard again. Logan often mentioned the man, who was absent during her sparring. "The general won't let anyone hurt her."

Logan scoffed. "You don't know the general." As if to punctuate this statement, the white-haired general disarmed Raena with a flick of his blade, then darted behind her before she could react.

Logan tensed, his hand on his sword hilt. There was a raw energy about him that Toben only sensed on this field, like the fervor expressed in battle... or in bed. If Toben didn't know better, he'd think Logan wished to take the place of Raena's bodyguard. The closeness to her bedchamber would come with the job; maybe he wanted to save her from everyone but himself.

Feeling a little imbalanced, Toben forced his gaze off of Logan, just as Raena conceded the match with a flirtatious bat of her eyelashes. Won't be long before she's fucking hat old man, he thought, if the two aren't twisting bedsheets already.

The image impressed itself in his mind, and he adjusted his belt again. He chanced another look at Logan, wondering if he might be thinking along the same lines. Logan's scowl was impressive as he watched Raena leave the field, and he didn't even blink until she was safely back in the castle. But even then, the man's spirits did not seem to lift. For all he disliked her, the woman filled up his mind.

"Well," Toben said, to fill the thick silence, "I'd better get back to your armor." As an officer's tentmate, he had unofficially become a sort of page for the man. This included polishing Logan's armor and weapons.

"Mind you get the filigree," Logan groused, and a small thrill went through Toben. This wasn't unusual—unlike most people, he liked to be told what to do—but there was something in Logan's brooding eyes that made the order seem darker.

Toben felt his ears heat. His erection over Raena had just been subsiding. It seemed to be reversing course now.

"I'll do that, Sir," he blurted. Trying not to think about the sudden urges in his gut, he added, "Anything else?"

Logan glanced at him and growled, "Are you patronizing me, soldier?"

Toben swallowed as his pulse started jumping. "No, Sir. Just trying to be helpful."

"In that case," Logan said, clearly not believing a word of it, "how about you oil my gauntlets too?"

Toben nodded, eager to leave and do what he was told.

Logan narrowed his eyes. "Did you hear me, soldier? Repeat that shit back to me. Or maybe you'd prefer to clean privies?"

"I'll mind the filigree, sir," Toben rushed out, feeling hot. "I'll oil your gauntlets, sir. 'Til they shine."

Logan straightened. "See that you do."

But as Toben scurried off, he could feel Logan's eyes at his back. His penis seemed to get harder, not softer.

What is going on? he thought, before shaking his head. Nothing was going on. He was horny over Raena, and Logan's presence was just—just what? Impossible to ignore?

It wasn't the first time this had happened, and it didn't matter. Seeing another man's raw desire often had this effect. Toben had gotten erect over much dumber things. He'd once gotten hard when he watched a horse eat a carrot.

So this was a fluke. A silly trick of his body.

But it wasn't gone by the time he reached the tent.

And it didn't leave afterward, either. When he started working with Logan's breastplate, rubbing wax into the metal to shine it, the circular movement of the waxing triggered a seedy part of his mind. When he pressed hard into the filigree, the swaying lines dried his mouth. He found himself thinking wet, nameless thoughts.

Looking out through hooded eyes, he glanced at the tent flap. Logan was on leave today, so he'd be gone awhile. What-ever was causing this need, Toben felt like expending it. He transferred the waxing rag to his non-dominant hand.

With his left, he fingered the notch of his belt, pulling it open, his fingertips feathering onto the fleshy head of his penis. He didn't stop waxing as he caressed himself, starting slow and easy, whispering over the warm ridge and then down his damp shaft. Mind you get the filigree, he reminded himself, but he wasn't talking about the breastplate anymore.

He sighed as he rubbed near the top of his balls, while he worked wax into the breastplate's engraving. The armor seemed to get hazy behind the film of his pleasure, and his gaze slipped to his next task, Logan's gauntlets. He stopped waxing and touched them, trying to remember where the oil was. His hand drifted over the rounded segments of metal—

"Working hard, I see," Logan said.

Toben yelped and spun, knocking a gauntlet onto the ground in his haste. He nearly fell in the small space, but managed to plop onto his cot, his pants loose but mercifully closed as he sat.

"Sir!" he gasped, hastily pulling his belt back through its loops. "This isn't—"

"What it looks like?" Logan asked.

Toben ran his tongue through his mouth, but he found neither saliva, nor words. Logan didn't seem to be angry, but there was that same disapproval he'd worn at the field.

Scowling, Logan bent over the disorganized pile of his things and rifled around in one of his canvas bags. Then he pulled out a bottle and tossed it at Toben. Toben dropped it and had to pick it up off the floor.

"There's your armor oil," Logan said. "Use it."

Toben felt his brown face go sunburn-red. He started to stand, but Logan straightened with such sharpness and precision that Toben found himself sitting again.

"I said," Logan growled, "use it."

The command went straight to Toben's head, and his penis reacted, even before the rest of him did. He felt it strain against his breeches, and he wanted to scream. This was not the time to get horny in front of an officer. Logan might think he was gay—

Then the order hit him. Use it. He looked at the bottle of oil in his hand, and realized it had no label. The bottle looked decorative, the glass etched with a pattern. Mouth hanging open, he unscrewed the lid. The pink scent of flowers wafted out.

He looked up to see Logan raise an eyebrow and back away

to lean on a tent pole. He crossed his arms and watched to see what Toben would do.

"Is—is that an order?" Toben said. This was not armor oil.

"Do you want it to be?" Logan asked.

Yes, Toben thought. His dick jumped, tense and eager. Five hells take me, but I want this. Yes.

Logan's eyebrow descended as if the mystery was now solved. "Use the oil, you damn maggot," he said after a moment. "Or are you planning to keep an officer waiting?"

Slowly, heart thudding, Toben pulled his shirt tails aside, exposing himself and waiting to be yelled at. But Logan only watched him—his eyes, not his dick—as he spread oil on his hand, then his penis.

"That's right," Logan said. "Shine that baby up. I want to see it gleam."

Toben held the man's gaze as he moistened his penis. Then he closed his fist on his shaft. The first stroke was a slow movement, testing. His knuckles pressed into the flesh by his balls. Then he rose languorously up the full length of his cock.

For Toben, it was not a short journey.

Toben knew he had advantages that other men did not— nothing incredible, but something to be proud of. But as his fat head bulged between his forefinger and thumb, Logan still only watched Toben's eyes.

His flesh quivered, and he knew that if he went even a single smidge faster, he'd be spritzing all over this tent.

"Is that all you got, maggot?" Logan asked.

"Yes, sir," he tried to say, pumping. "It's all I got, sir," he repeated.

"You think a big sword makes you special?"

"No, sir. It doesn't make me special, sir."

"You think you're better than me, don't you. Because my sword is smaller?"

"No, sir. You can use yours better, sir."

The answer rolled off his tongue without his even knowing. He paused his stroking to see how Logan would react.

Logan rolled his eyes. "You're as bad as the rest of them. Another squirming little suck-up." He rose off the tent pole and shrugged his shoulders. "Pathetic little worms, all of you." He worked angrily at his belt, yanking it out of its loops. Toben was sure he would use it to strike him.

"You know what worms are good for?" Logan said, snapping the belt taut. "Eating shit. Are you a worm, Toben? Or are you a man?"

Toben watched in awe as Logan put a hand inside his own breeches and closed his fist inside. Then Logan stepped closer, until his crotch was only a hand's width from Toben's face. He could see the bulge, but nothing more. Five gods, did he want to see more?

"I said, are you a man, Toben?" Logan repeated. "Or are you a dirty little worm?"

Toben's fist tightened. Worm. Worm. I'm a dirty little worm. "I'm a man," he managed. Was that the answer Logan wanted?

"No, sir. I'm a man, sir. Repeat that shit back to me, maggot."

"No, sir. I'm a man, sir."

"No you're not. Look at you. Can't even oil up a gauntlet. Listen to that awful squeak."

He meant the sucking noise of the strokes. Tha-whip. Tha-whip. Toben felt his body melt under Logan's pressure, felt himself expand like a dough under heat.

"I'm sorry, sir. I'll do it right next time, sir. I'll oil up the gauntlet without squeaking, sir."

Logan's hand shifted in his pants, and flesh nudged the

fabric aside. A deep brown head with wrinkled edges winked out.

"Oh gods," Toben shuddered.

"Like what you see?" Logan asked.

Toben said nothing, overwhelmed. He knew what came next. He knew what he'd be told to do.

"I'll give you one more chance," Logan said. He shook his penis free. "See this? It's my sword. And it needs a good spit-shine. Do you think you have what it takes?"

Toben nodded, feverish. He'd sped up again—fipfipfip.

"Slow down," Logan said. "If you get wax on my pants, you'll be licking it off."

"Yes, sir. I'll slow down, sir." Toben slowed. "I'll spit-shine your sword, sir."

"Good. Now get polishing. I don't want to be here forever."

Logan put his free hand on Toben's head, and pulled him in.

Toben had never put his mouth on a dick before. He'd never imagined it was something he would want. But as the flesh met his tongue, his fist froze on his shaft. All he could think about was the shape on his tongue.

Logan's grip hardened at the back of his head. Even that small touch was an order, a clear demand. Toben tried to swallow, pulling the penis deeper. He tasted the same salt he used to smell on himself.

"Are you a fast learner, Toben?" Logan asked, his voice finally husking. Toben nodded, making the penis slide on his tongue. Yes, sir. I'm a fast learner, sir.

He realized he'd forgotten to breathe, and he drew a sharp breath through his nose. His tongue curled, outlining shapes in his mind.

"Good," Logan said. "Then this'll be a crash lesson. You get one minute to learn to keep your teeth out of the way. Then you're going to sit there and take my dick 'til I'm done."

Toben nodded, raising his free hand to grip Logan around his hip bone for leverage, pressing his thumb into the giving flesh at his base. Toben bobbed closer, guided by the hand in his hair. He cocked his head to keep his teeth off the skin.

Logan groaned, his fingers forming a fist. But he didn't push. Not yet.

Toben turned his neck, puffed his cheeks, worked the angles. Learned what it was like to be a woman on her knees. He found a path for the penis that caught in his throat without risking the sharp edges of his teeth.

"Sloppy," Logan said, the same way he'd talked about Raena. "You call this a spit-shine," he stated.

It wasn't a question. It was a passing insult with no force. Toben could feel the man quivering from the need to go faster, from the need to fuck something right now.

Toben swelled with desire. He was just a quick fuck. He was the Raena that this man couldn't have.

Toben popped off, his chest fluttering. "I'm ready, sir," he exhaled.

Logan gripped Toben's head with both hands and put one foot on his cot. "Don't make a sound, maggot. I don't want to think of you."

Toben leaned closer. "Yes, sir."

Logan thrust.

He went with a speed and ferocity that Toben only used when they lost control. The gag reflex came first, his throat blocking and unblocking, and Toben's eyes watered as he tried not to make sounds. It was useless, of course, with flesh rampaging through his mouth, with his jaw wide open and slick with saliva. He made wet nauseous half-coughs, his penis rigid from memory. How many times had he paid a woman to do this? And he was so pathetic that he did it for free?

He gripped Logan's hips with both hands now as the man thrust in rage, the same frenzied fucking Toben used before coming. Logan breathed heavily, almost growling; Toben felt his raw need. He was a replacement, a stand-in, a simple release. A little maggot only good for one thing.

The thought made his dick shiver, his own orgasm hovering, even though he wasn't touching himself. He was a tool with a man's dick riding his useless tongue. He was just following orders. He was sad and pathetic.

"Am I good enough now?" he heard someone say, and it took a second before he realized it was Logan. The words mirrored his own thoughts, reflecting the opposite image. "Five gods, look what you made me do...."

Toben nodded, gripping the other man harder. His throat had grown used to the oppressive presence inside it. Jaw locking, he angled himself to take the dick without moving. In and out, wet and slide, feel the animal need, the long heat and the springy flesh, oh—

Logan swore and exploded inside Toben's mouth, a rush of salt and a strange, intense heat. Toben clamped his lips down and pressed his forehead closer, thinking dimly that he should want to escape. Instead he put a spare fist on himself while Logan jerked into his forehead, cum and spit dribbling down off his chin.

Toben masturbated so fast that for each time Logan spurted, he got in three strokes on himself. His superior officer groaned belatedly, his fists loosening in Toben's hair. Toben thought about swallowing—about how small it might make him. He sucked the ejaculate down his throat.

The cum roiled in his stomach, and then built in his core. It unfurled in his balls, and then burst.

Toben moaned in release, the sound muffled by the soft penis still ensconced in his mouth. He pressed his cheek to Logan's crotch and forgot himself as the cool air met the jumping head of his penis.

Logan stepped back suddenly, looking sweaty and pale, leaving Toben to lean on empty air. The officer staggered into the tent pole, and the two men looked at each other. Exhausted, and a little surprised.

The rush of the encounter faded almost instantly. Toben expected to be dressed down and disparaged within moments—

But Logan's confidence was no longer in evidence.

Logan looked down as Toben spurted a last time, a feeble budding of white at his tip. "Shit," he said. He tucked himself back into his pants. Toben did the same, and Logan said again, "Shit."

Toben wiped his mouth with his arm, waiting for the shame to wash over him, but it wouldn't come. The full dream of the blow job resolved into reality. He couldn't seem to draw enough breath.

But the silence. The horror. Logan was staring straight ahead. Toben realized the man had never done this before either. He realized that they were the same.

And he saw Logan slipping. Saw his knees giving out. If Toben didn't do something, this would never repeat. He'd never get to do this again.

"Well done, sir," he blurted. Logan met his eyes, wild. "You did a great job, sir. She would have liked it."

Logan stared at him. "What?"

"Raena would have liked it."

He expected to be yelled at. But he knew what he'd seen now. He'd been a tool of this man's release.

"How the fuck would you know?" Logan said, without rancor.

"She likes power, sir. Haven't you seen the general? The way she looks at him when he overcomes her?"

Logan scoffed. "You don't see her like I do. She hates losing."

"Maybe. But she likes power too."

Logan sank to the ground, which heartened Toben. Keep him talking. Make him see it. Or else we won't do this again.

"Powerful women don't like weak men," Toben rambled. "I would know. I'm one of them. If she ever fucked me, it would be out of pity." Five gods, how he craved a woman's pity.

But that wasn't Logan. Logan wasn't like him. They were opposites. That's why this had worked.

"I'm not—with men," Logan tried to say.

"Me neither. But a mouth is a mouth."

Logan looked up, and Toben could see shame in his eyes. He was trying to let it in, trying to darken all this pleasure.

For once in his life, Toben would take control.

He stood and crossed the room and lifted Logan by his collar. The bigger man's eyebrows rose in surprise as Toben looked up at him.

"Look," Toben said, "we're going to do this again. Every fucking time that you see her and want her. Your own hands aren't enough, are they? Or you wouldn't have done this. So you're going to take me out back like a paid whore and fuck me."

He wondered for a moment what he was offering. But he figured he'd try anything once.

Toben let Logan go. "You're going to make me feel worthless, like she makes you feel. And I'm going to make you feel like the biggest thing in the world."

Logan released a shuddering breath, his dark eyes still wide.

"Now repeat that shit back to me," Toben said. "Sir."

SIX

A STOLEN THING

TRIGGERS: MF, INNOCENCE FETISH, FAKING DESIRE.
COMPANION BOOK: THE HEART OF TOUCH.
SPOILERS: NONE.

W hen the time came for me to see my first penis, I
thought I was ready. I wasn't.

"Why are you so nervous?" Tallin asked me, while I paced
the front hall waiting for my suitor. The question made me stop
to look at my guard. Tallin rarely spoke, and we both
knew why.

We weren't alone, however; another guard was there. So I
settled for an innocuous response: "Isn't it normal for a girl to be
nervous before she meets a suitor?" I asked.

Tallin glanced at the other guard, Hannis. The much-older
man rolled his eyes. The two of them stood to either side of the
front door, waiting to play my escort when my suitor came
knocking. There was a temporary butler hovering somewhere
as well, probably serving my mother some tea. Mother could

only afford to hire such servants for special functions, and she'd get as much use out of them as she could.

"Well," Tallin said, "yes, I guess most girls would be nervous. But it's not like you'll marry the guy."

I swallowed. *Oh yes I will.* Mother would skin me alive if I didn't.

Hannis stepped into the conversation then. "Not your place to comment, boy," he groused. "Miss Eren here is no common woman. It's different for old families like hers."

And it's even more different if those families are dirt broke, I thought. *Especially if their only child is a homely one, without magic.*

Tallin glanced worriedly at me, then blushed and averted his bright green gaze. I hated that he was here, that he would witness my shame. I only hoped he wouldn't witness *all* of it.

"But he's... so much older," Tallin said, his voice small now.

"And a hells-of-a lot richer, too," Harris huffed.

I swallowed at this, and adjusted my skirts, checking and rechecking every fold for wrinkles or dust. I started to pace again, using the action to keep from looking at Tallin. Tallin, tall and lanky and self-conscious, with eyes that always lingered, and a smile that lingered longer. I used to count the hours between his hirings, to imagine and re-imagine and re-re-imagine all the things he might do if he got me alone.

But if he ever did that, he'd lose his job at the guard agency, and I'd lose the "flower" my mother thought was so precious.

A knock sounded at the door then, and we waited, tense. Tallin was watching his feet, gripping the pike he always held to make him look menacing despite having such a kissable face.

What about a guard, Mother? Can't I marry a guard?

A guard?! What kind of money do they have? They can't save this family, Eren. Only a rich man can save us.

While we waited for the butler to scurry out of hiding and

pretend he'd always been in our service, I looked about the grand entrance hall of my family's mansion. The walls were paneled in luxuriant mahogany, the lamps glowing with Tinkered blue magelight, the crystal shards of the chandelier tinkling softly in a draft that no one had fixed. In the wake of my mother's illness and my father's gambling, that chandelier was now the most expensive object we owned, second only to the dress I was wearing. The house, the crystal, and the tight-fitting silk... these things represented the last coins of a failing country lordship.

And if I didn't snag Cezar Scan *today*, on this very walk, then I'd inherit nothing but dust.

I can't do this, Mother. I can't do this—

Of course you can, darling. You're such a fast learner. Now do as I do, and you shall be fine.

"How may I help you?" the butler said, and I jumped. When had he walked past me? I must be losing it. But every time I pictured my mother back on her knees, a part of my brain seemed to shut off.

"I'm here to escort the Lady Eren around the grounds," said the ardent voice of a thirty-two-year-old man. Cezar Scan, father and widower; wealthy surveyor; and twelve years my senior. "I believe Lady Ronna is aware of my coming?"

"One moment please," the butler said primly, and shut the door in Cezar's face. Another ploy to make the rich man feel like *lesser* here—as if he'd add quite a lot of money to his estates, if he could only coax this young woman into marriage.

I've set it all up for you, darling, Mother had said. *He believes he roped your father into allowing this meeting. He'll already want you, from the start.*

I tried to catch the butler's eye as he stood close by, tapping his foot to count out the seconds. He'd make Cezar wait, of course—more illusion. I almost wished Mother would come down, but she was too weak to walk anymore—and nothing she could say would make me any less nervous.

I caught movement from the corner of my eye, and turned in time to see Tallin licking his lips. The butler's act must be making my situation more clear.

He met my eyes as if to say, *So it's hopeless?*

Finally the butler opened the door wide, and any other girl would have straightened her spine and thrown back her shoulders as she was revealed to her suitor. But not me. My back and shoulders were already in position. Such things were a natural state for me; after a lifetime of training in perfection, I could manage such poise in my sleep.

Still, I wasn't all that beautiful, so it pleased me to see Cezar perk up at the sight of me. The hair extensions, meticulously curled into highly sought-after ringlets, must be doing their work. That and the makeup. And the dress. And my gaze.

Smile like this. Do as I do.

I smiled like my mother had shown me, dipping my head and looking up through my lashes.

"Hello, Sir Scan," I said in a soft, unsure voice. A voice that said, *I'm so nervous. And excited. I've never had a suitor before.*

Cezar was handsome, at least, thank the Feeling Queen. Tall and broad-shouldered, a little pudgy but still muscular, with a straight jaw and a finger-thin beard. He clapped his fat hands at the sight of me, his vivid eyes wide as the day. There were as blue as Tallin's were green.

"Lady Eren, how lovely you look!" Cezar enthused. He bent to hold an arm out to me, and I took it tentatively. "And such a lovely day to take you about the grounds. I'm told you have duck pond, is that true?"

Yes, but the ducks are all wild now. We had to slaughter the pet ones.

I leaned into him eagerly. "Oh, yes! Would you like to see it?"

He patted my hand on his arm and smiled warmly. "Lead the way."

I did so, the two guards following us at a fair distance as we stepped off the wraparound porch and traversed the gravel path around the side of the manse. As far as Cezar knew, Tallin and Hannis were there to ensure nothing untoward occurred between the suitor and the suited; a lady's "precious flower" was still worth something, after all.

"So tell me," Cezar said as the vast ground came into view— the only person still on permanent staff was our gardener— "how does such a pretty lady occupy her spare time? Surely not with old farts like me."

Flattery. The word burst to my mind—one of my mother's commands. *And giggles. He will like giggles.*

I giggled. "You're not old," I said, and I blushed. My mother had trained me to do it on cue. It involved picturing a man naked to trigger the blood rush. In my case, I always chose Tallin.

"You flatter me," Cezar said aptly, "but I know the truth. Your father could hardly bear to let me meet you. He's very much hoping you won't be taken with me. And I'm sure you have many younger men to choose from."

You don't like the younger boys. Older men fascinate you. But don't say those things outright—just insinuate them.

I fought the urge to look back at the house, to check to see if the butler were sneaking out the side door, as planned. "Oh, well, my father *is* wise," I said, looking away, my arm loosening in his.

For a long, tense moment, he said nothing. Then he leaned close, a private grin lighting his face. "You say that like you don't believe it."

I giggled, a hand to my mouth this time. *He's so funny.
Laugh at his jokes.*

"You mustn't tell him," I said lowly.

"Oh, I wouldn't dream of it."

"It's just that, well...."

"Yes?"

He was so close to me now, and the duck pond was nearing.
Oh, this game. Mother knew it so well. He was acting exactly as
she had said he would; her sources on him must have been
right.

"I think that young men are so dull," I blurted.

Cezar started and straightened away from me, and I rushed
out, "They just—well, they—they don't really know what
they're doing, do they? Always waving their swords around and
talking big when they've got nothing but their father's name.
Half of them have no skill beyond drinking and horse riding.
And you *know* there's only one thing on their mind...."

At this I stopped, blushing again, picturing Tallin in all his
glory, muscular and bronzed and leaning over me, nudging the
shoulder strap of my fine dress aside....

Cezar belted out a laugh. "Oh, my dear Eren, you have it
right! I was no better as a young man, myself." He shook his
head. "And my wife, rest her soul, fell for it, poor thing. But I
see you are more discerning than she."

What kind of man would say that about his late wife? I
thought, but shoved the thought away just as quickly. "Was she
very pretty? Your wife," I asked him.

"Oh, yes. But she was a firebomb. I'm looking for something
a little easier, this time around."

Easier. Easy. A keyword. My mother had taught me so
many.

"I can be easy," I said softly—not seductively, never seductively. Every hint, every flirt, it all had to be innocent. Because

that's what Cezar Scan wanted. It's what he asked for, when he went to the brothels.

Cezar looked at me and raised an eyebrow, and I gasped as if only just realizing my innuendo. "I mean—I—that is to say—"

He patted my hand again, laughing in a resonant way. The sound was actually... pleasing. For the first time, I felt a little excitement.

"I know what you meant, milady," he said. "Have no fear. Now is this the famous duck pond?"

We had now reached the sunlit water, and were walking abreast of it, on a pathway pinned between the water's edge and a thick stand of trees. The time was fast approaching—any moment now. I had only a few seconds before the last act began.

I pointed at a random duck, a wild mallard. "Oh, look!" I said. "That's Lucky. He's my favorite."

"Lucky?" Cezar asked, no doubt wondering what set that particular duck apart from the rest of them. Nothing at all, not that I could see. "Why do you call him that?"

I leaned my arm against his. "Because he only shows up when good things happen," I said. "So today is going to be a good—"

BOOM.

I jumped and screeched, very believably, as I was not faking. Cezar reacted even better than I could have hoped, gripping me by the arms and shoving me behind him, putting himself between me and the smoke across the water. Hannis and Tallin were turning too, pikes up, and Hannis—more aware of the plan than Tallin—slapped his younger partner and sent Tallin scurrying off toward the smoke. Tallin never even thought to look back, never even considered what might happen next.

Hannis jogged up to us. "What is it, man?" Cezar asked him.

"I don't know, but I'll find out, sir. Will you two be all right alone for a few minutes?"

"Alone? Are you mad?" Cezar asked, his voice rising. "What if it's some sort of attack—"

"I know, sir, but we are short-staffed today. A guard's wife is in childbirth, you see, and I can't let young Tallin go alone—"

I stepped around Cezar. "It's fine, Hannis. We'll hide in the trees here until you return." I looked up at Cezar. "I know the woods well. Don't worry. I just couldn't bear it if Tallin were hurt, or if he couldn't stop someone coming to my father, or if—" my voice raised, and I faced Hannis again, trying to force my face to lose all its color.

Hannis glanced at Cezar, who nodded him forward, and off Hannis ran to face the unknowable threat. Later, it would be revealed as a disgruntled ex-servant. In reality, it had been the act of a highly-paid—if temporary—butler.

"Just here," I told Cezar, leading him onto the first path I found. It was true that I knew these woods by heart, and I had carved many of their paths myself. This one led to a great oak, so large it had killed off any other trees trying to grow beneath it. I led Cezar to the tree, hiding us behind it. The area was open and exposed, and yet hidden from the pond by a thick wall of brush. I wondered if Mother had gone so far as to ask the gardener not to prune the brush this past week; I wouldn't put it past her to attend to such details.

With Cezar's hand in both of mine, and my heart pounding, I said, "What do you suppose that was?"

He pulled me close to him, embracing me. I curled my arms in and lay my head on his chest as he said, "Don't worry. Your father's men will take care of it."

I nodded against him, ready to force a quiver through my

body, but finding instead that the quiver was already there. I knew what was coming, and it frightened and excited me. Perhaps it couldn't be Tallin... but perhaps it would feel exhilarating all the same.

I looked up in startlement and backed away from him. "Oh! I'm sorry. That's most untoward of me."

Cezar's gaze was soft... and something else. His eyes flicked around the clearing and he smiled again. "Nonsense. You're frightened. The least I can do is hold you; the guards could hardly fault me for that."

Hesitating, I nodded and drew close to him again, leaning my head against his shoulder with one of my hands held in his. With his free hand, he ran his fingers it through my false ringlets, gentle and exploratory. My breathing tightened, and I spread the fingers of my own free hand, on his chest.

"There, there," he said, his voice rougher now. His hand drifted out of my hair to my collar, down to my shoulder, down my spine to my lower back. I swallowed my next breath, an audible hitch. His touch slowed, but neither one of us pulled away.

"Perhaps I should go," Cezar said.

"No. Please don't go."

"You're right. This is untoward...."

He trailed off, and we were silent. I counted the seconds. *Do as I do.*

"They'll be back any moment," I said. They wouldn't be.

"Yes," he croaked.

More silence.

I leaned away from him, let him go, and rubbed my arms, my gaze always locked on the ground. I made it clear that there was something I wanted to say, but that it was very hard to say it.

"My dear, what is it?" he said softly. I was not used to

hearing desire in another person's voice, but I recognized it now, in his.

I drew a steadying breath, my chest rising. The dress was a tight one, prim, hiding most of my curves, if I could be said to have any at all. But the fabric was thin, and I trailed my fingers up my stomach and over my breasts to my throat.

"I feel... so hot," I exhaled.

His mouth opened slightly as he considered this. "Maybe you should unbutton your collar?"

I nodded distractedly, still looking away as I opened my collar, showing him the skin of my neck, my throat, and then my collarbone. I let him stare at the bare, forbidden flesh for a long moment.

Then I turned my gaze on his penis.

I tried not to be obvious, but of course I was obvious, especially once I actually looked. I'd played out this act many times with my mother, but I'd never actually *looked* at a man's crotch.

But I did it now, and saw a significant shape waiting for me, pressing against both layers of his trousers. My chest flipped, my pulse raced. I'd never *looked* before. And there it was, straining to meet me.

Cezar lowered his hand, his fingers brushing across the shape of his manhood. Would he make me ask? Or would he offer? In these supposed few minutes where we were alone?

He took a chance. "Do you... want to see it?"

I still didn't look at him. I couldn't. I was too embarrassed, too horny, too innocent. All the things he wanted me to be.

I ran my hands down the front of my dress, to get the sweat off them. "Yes," I breathed.

Out of the corner of my eye, I saw him look toward the smoke, or what little of it he could see through the trees. Judging discovery to be worth the risk, he tugged on his belt. The leather end slipped through the buckle, then out through the metal. The pants hung loose, and he reached one hand inside them, pushing them down, and pushing something else out.

I didn't have to pretend now. I was *seeing* it. A round hunk of brown flesh with a pinprick hole in the center. His hand around it, forcing it closer to me.

"Oh," I said. I felt like I might faint.

His voice was tenuous, hungry. "Do you like it?"

I bit my lip, my hands fiddling. I nodded.

"Do you want to touch it?" he asked.

I waited a beat, then stepped closer, so that his gaze could travel down my open collar to the tops of my breasts. I reached down and prodded the bulbous tip. The flesh gave to my touch. His breath caught.

"Lower," he rasped, taking his hand off himself. I slid my fingers past the soft head to the harder flesh beneath, hotter than I had ever expected. My curiosity set my nerves afire as I circled the shaft with both hands and squeezed.

"Oh, Lady *Eren*," he whispered.

"Is it... am I doing it right?"

He fingered the open flap of my collar, then popped out the next button. "Harder. Up and down."

I obeyed, gripping him and pulling and then pushing. It was a smooth ride, the flesh loose on the muscle, bunching up at the top when I pulled, and the bottom when I pushed. He pressed his forehead to mine, and his fingers worked faster, until the fabric whispered away from my nipples.

"Cezar—"

He gripped my breasts and I stopped stroking in surprise; his fingers sank into me, his thumbs depressing my nipples. My flesh was hard too, pebbled with need. I felt the craving deep inside me, the same craving I usually felt only in fantasy, only in touching myself in the dark of the night.

"You're perfect," he said. "Don't stop."

I began again in earnest. Faster, faster. With one hand I explored, finding his testicles; I cupped them as he pinched my nipples. My vagina was afire now, my resolutions all fading. My mother had warned me this would happen, that even just the sight of him would make my senses flee.

I hadn't believed her. Not a man as old as Cezar. Not while Tallin was alive did I think I might want someone else. But I would have taken anyone in that moment, had they offered.

Cezar let go of my breasts and kissed my neck, my throat, my chest. As he sucked my nipples into his mouth, I gasped, but he was already lifting my skirts, gathering them.

"No," I said feebly. *Yes.* "No...."

His mouth popped off me and he trailed kissed to my ear. "I won't go inside. I just want to touch you."

I swung my chest against his, my bare skin to his coat buttons. I let go of his penis, my arms encircling his neck.

And he touched me, his fingers like sparks in the darkness. I moaned in real pleasure, hooking one leg on his hip as he swung me around and pressed my back to the tree.

Then he was kissing my neck, sucking so hard that I felt the bruise coming even as the pleasure swelled in my lower stomach. He rubbed me on the outside, on my trigger-place, between the tender folds at the front of me; but then his fingers dipped inside all my wetness and I moaned senselessly, arching against him.

His touch faded away, and in that brief moment I felt alarm and regained just enough presence to understand what was happening when his penis rubbed up against me.

But I wanted it. Surely, it wouldn't matter. Surely, if he just had a taste, he'd want more—

If you give it to him, you won't be special. My mother's words flared in my head. *He can always find another woman.*

But he can't always find another virgin, and not one who wants him so badly.

"No," I managed. "No, stop."

He fumbled, touching me again, with both his fingers and his penis. I shuddered, fighting the desire to sink down on him. *He can always find another woman.*

"Not like—th-this," I croaked.

"I want you. I love you."

The absurdity of this declaration made my eyes widen, my sight clear. I tensed. "Not before marriage."

His finger dropped away, and he gripped himself, his penis pumping back and forth between my folds. My mouth opened, as if I were perpetually inhaling new breath. His head was rubbing across *that* place now—

"Oh. *Oh—*"

I jerked in his arms, up and away from his penis as the orgasm swept over me, more intense than I'd ever felt on my own. His fingers dipped inside me, and I felt the pulse of my own muscles against them.

"You're so tight," he growled. "Let me come in you."

"No...."

"Let me fuck you wide open," he said.

The words should have made me sick, but they had the opposite effect. As the orgasm waned, I wanted *more*. His fingers weren't enough. I needed something thicker.

"I can't," I murmured. "It's not proper—"

"They'll be back any second."

"I know—"

He backed away then, leaving me slumped against the tree, my skirts falling and my breasts hanging out. He was holding himself, his hand working expertly. It occurred to me then how much experience I lacked. He had done this hundreds, maybe thousands of times.

"Don't you want it?" he said, his penis jumping with each pump. He seemed to be thrusting it at me. "Don't you want to feel it?"

The burning was back. *Yes.* If I pulled him against me—if I clung to his hips with my legs, threw my head back....

I dropped like a stone and tugged on the bunched fabric under his stroking hands, yanking him toward me. He groaned in surprise as his flesh slid between my teeth and rubbed my throat.

"How does it taste?" he said, with something cruel in his voice.

It tasted like sweat. My body was cooling. I murmured my hunger, though the hunger was gone.

"You ever had your mouth on a dick before, girl?"

I shook my head no. I hadn't. He put one hand on the tree above my head and started to thrust forward. I gagged, but he didn't stop. The ride became a bit smoother, a bit easier, though it was harder to control where his penis went as his thrusts grew erratic. *No teeth,* my mother had instructed, showing me the stance, on her knees. *Suck until your cheeks hurt, swing your tongue about when you think of it, but mostly just keep it off the teeth.*

If it hadn't been so new, I might have felt violated. But the experience was fresh, exciting in its way. His spare hand—the one that had so lovingly caressed my hair—was now gripping me by the scalp. I was afraid he'd tear out my extensions, and find out how short and pitiful my hair really was.

Instead he forced my head forward, made me suck deeper. Springy flesh plunged across my tongue to my throat and back.

Then heat, salt, groaning as his penis leapt from my mouth and back into his hand. I gasped in air as hot wet sprang across my bare chest; I felt the ejaculate before I saw it, pulsing out of his head as he aimed it at me.

It was gross, possessive, but my training ran deep. I threw my head back and pretended to enjoy it as Cezar Scan marked me as his.

THAT NIGHT, after Cezar made his offers and my father faked his disdain all of the official papers were signed—after all of that, I snuck out of my bedroom, through a window and out onto my roof.

I had never done this before, but the fall of night had electrified me. I climbed down a trellis with more confidence than I'd ever felt in my life, and I crossed the open courtyard to the servant's house. He would be here tonight; my Mother had paid him to do it. Anything to keep Sir Cezar under the impression that Lady Eren was the catch of his life.

I knew which window to tap because I'd watched it so many times. Dreamed of doing this *so many times*.

The window swung open on too-creaky hinges. "Lady Eren?" Tallin asked. "What—?"

I kissed him, sank my fingers into his hair and kissed him until his resistance melted and he taught me how to use my tongue in new ways. This was something I *hadn't* given Cezar in that forest, something that was still raw and new.

But it was something I *would* give Cezar, eventually. When we were married, he would have everything.

Not everything, I thought. There was still one more new thing. One thing I could steal back from my husband, and instead give to the boy that I loved.

I broke the kiss. "Let me in," I whispered.

And after kissing me once more, Tallin did.

SEVEN

CONTRACTUAL

TRIGGERS: MFF, FIRST TIME, LESBIAN.
COMPANION BOOKS: THE MARIGOLD ROOM, THE
MORNING AGENT.
SPOILERS: SLIGHT.

S henni Null had not expected to stay a virgin this long—if
that was what she actually *was*. Gods knew she'd already
had plenty of sex. It just hadn't been with a *man*.

"Relax," Orra said, pressing down harder on her shoulders.
The two sat in the pool of cushions and silk beside Orra's
gigantic bathtub—the place she tended to retire to with her
clients, after bathing. Just *thinking* about that made Shenni
burn with envy—even thought she was the one getting the back
rub right now, in a dress that barely counted as clothing.

As usual, Orra proved herself attuned to Shenni's thoughts,
and leaned forward from behind to nuzzle her neck and peel
her sheer collar away from her neck. The fabric was light as a
lover's breath, and Shenni shivered as Orra's lips found her bare
skin, at that lovely place just over her collarbone.

Orra continued to rub the stress and fear from her shoulders. "It's going to be fine," she purred.

Shenni couldn't help it; she tensed again. Any minute now, that goofy door guard was going to knock on her door and step through, and she'd have to spread her legs for him. She had nothing against the man himself; he was nice enough, maybe even handsome to some people. She merely had absolutely *zero* attraction. No attraction, and no choice.

"Are you sure I can't have some wine?" Shenni asked, as Orra's hold loosened. The older woman pushed her braids away from the back of her neck, and ran the tip of her nose along Shenni's hairline. Shenni quivered—she had no choice in *that,* either—but the usual lust didn't come. Not even as Orra pulled the top of her dress clean off her shoulders, her fingertips trailing down Shenni's bare spine.

"You're going to want to feel it," Orra breathed into the shadows behind her left ear. "All of it. Everything...."

"No, actually, I won't. I'm a lesbian, remember?"

Orra turned her chin with a fingertip and kissed her on the mouth. "Just trust me, Shen. It's a whole different feeling." She drew closer, twisting Shenni around, putting her mouth to hers and spreading her wide. Orra's tongue was a dervish for several heart-pounding moments, until finally, she broke away.

Shenni found herself on her back, the larger woman above her. Orra's breasts hung within kissing distance. Now, Shenni *did* feel the lust.

"Why do you think I've held off on using toys for so long?" Orra said, shrugging one shoulder so that her unbuttoned dress could slip off. One of her enormous breasts broke free of the fabric, and Shenni felt a twitch in her groin.

"Toys," she echoed, barely aware of the word. She reached out with both hands and drew Orra's huge, coal-black nipple to her mouth. Orra gasped theatrically as Shenni suckled her soft flesh to a point. Soon they were both panting, and Orra was pulling Shenni's sheer dress down over her small breasts and thin hips. Once she'd gotten it past Shenni's vagina, her hand paused, and her fingertips brushed against the fine hairs between Shenni's legs.

"Toys," she repeated, over the wet sounds of Shenni's mouth. She parted Shenni's lips with her fingers. "Right here."

Shenni broke her mouth off her lover. "I don't need toys," she said. "I have your mouth."

Orra laughed and prodded her lightly with a finger, making Shenni arch her back.

"I *do* have a good mouth," Orra admitted, dropping her breasts to both sides of Shenni's face. Shenni turned her face to unearth the second nipple. She had to give both breasts their equal attention....

"*But,*" Orra said, "you've never had dick before. Not even the kind made of wood. And once you've tried it, you'll want to try again. Having an orgasm around one... oh boy. You are in for something *delicious.*"

With that, Orra found her clit with two eager fingers, and started to circle and moisten. In Shenni's mouth, Orra's nipple was like a hard piece of candy. Shenni started to nibble; Orra sighed and leaned closer. Shenni was now drowning in flesh.

She's bigger than me. So much bigger than me. The thought made Shenni spread her legs wide.

"The most important thing," Orra exhaled, "is that it will feel *new.* Think of it like an experiment. Think of it like it was *us* who hired *him....* We're old women, bored women, we've been together too long. He's here to add some spice to our sex lives...."

Shenni gripped Orra's thick hips, sucking harder. She wanted nothing more than to grow old with Orra. The only good thing about this damn place was that she actually *might*. But they'd have to share each other... *dammit*. Shenni did not want to share.

"But first," Orra said, and Shenni made a small noise of protest as Orra pulled away, dragging her huge breasts down Shenni's chest, then her stomach. Shenni got grabby-hands as she watched the flesh go, her fingers tensing with the need to draw Orra back.

But Orra didn't waste time letting her try. Instead, she lowered her head and flicked out her tongue. Tears sprang to Shenni's eyes at the swift heat on her clitoris. It was always so *emotional,* when they did this. She hated Orra's tongue at the same time she loved it. She despised the organ as it swept clear up her vagina, sloppy and wide, like an animal cleaning another animal.

At the same time, she'd give anything to feel more of it... and Orra was happy to deliver. She started off with lopsided, inefficient licks, exactly the way Shenni liked it.

Blind King, Blind King, Shenni swore in her head. Her insides burned with need, her fists digging into the cushions as Orra tightened her movements, honed in on her nub, and took her ever closer to the edge.

QUINN WISE WAS NERVOUS, and yet hard as a rock. He was embarrassed that he was hard as a rock.

He'd been standing in front of this door for several minutes already, and not entirely by choice. But no one said no to Jorr Portent. Except maybe for his brother, Jaen.

Quinn shivered. Both men were terrifying. He'd dealt with them on and off for most of his life, but working directly under one of them—even if temporarily—was not something he wanted to repeat.

How much have you made from all these side jobs you've been doing? Jorr had asked him yesterday, when he'd been manning his post at the door of the House. It might have been a casual question, if it hadn't been Jorr. The Portent twins almost always *looked* casual, but Quinn had never seen them actually *mean* it.

But of course, Quinn had answered the question. Jorr's presence was enough to make him do it.

Good, Jorr had replied. *Take ten thousand out of that fund, and pay it straight to the crown. You're buying a Rose Contract tomorrow.*

Quinn swallowed, wishing his idiot erection would go away. He didn't *want* to want this. He hadn't *wanted* to squander his hard-earned personal cash. It was hard enough to have a life separate from his family wealth, without Jorr-Fuck-ing-Portent selling him virgins.

He quivered at the thought. *A virgin.* He'd had a few lovers by now—with a family name like his, why wouldn't he?—but they'd all been experienced women. For once, *he* would be the one without a clue.

A lesbian. A lesbian virgin.

He groaned aloud and knocked before he could reconsider. *She needs me to do this. I have to. That's all.*

But then why did he want it so much?

"Come in," a throaty voice called from within. He blinked. That was *Orra's* voice.

Steeling himself, he stepped through, catching a thin glimpse of the scene before hastily closing the door. He paused with his palm on the handle, and finally turned around.

Orra smiled at him, completely naked, on her hands and knees in the cushions. Beside her, Shenni—his assigned lover—

sat up, flushed, with a cut of silk wrapped around her. She was clearly naked as well.

"Hey, Quinn," Shenni said. Her voice was husky. He hadn't even been sure that she knew his name.

Orra laughed heavily, the sort of sound that hammers through tension rather than simply breaking it. She rose, drawing his eyes back to her ridiculously large breasts as she crossed the cushions toward him.

"I—I didn't—" he stammered as she began to strip off his coat.

"Didn't know this was a package deal?" she asked.

He shook his head. He'd just signed the papers.

Orra leaned closer, her palms on his shoulders. The closeness of those breasts made him even *more* nervous. He glanced at Shenni, whose flush had gone pale.

But when Orra spoke in his ear, the voice was deadly cold.

"You will be an absolute *gentleman*," she hissed, "or I will cut off your cock."

He felt the heat drain clear out of him, leaving nothing but fear and bewilderment. The words had been too low for Shenni to hear. All he could manage in reply was, "Yes, ma'am."

Orra nodded brightly to him, as if she had never uttered any threat in her life. Then she gallantly began to divest him of every last shred of his clothing. He was too afraid for his life to feel embarrassed when she removed his underclothes and exposed him as limp.

Well, that works, I suppose, he thought. He hadn't *wanted* to want Shenni, and now that he was afraid for his very penis, it appeared he had lost that desire.

He actually gulped. "Maybe I should go...."

Orra prodded him in the chest with a fingertip. "No. You stay. We do this." She smiled, but the smile was like stone. "You just follow my lead," she told him. It *clearly* was not a suggestion.

Quinn allowed himself to be dragged toward the cushions and yanked to his knees. He glanced at Shenni, trying to impart his regret to her, but she was looking at his crotch and biting her lip, holding the fabric ever tighter to her chest. She did not like what she saw, was not attracted to it. *It does get bigger,* he wanted to say.

But she wouldn't care for that either, would she?

She's a lesbian, Jorr had said. *She won't like it too much. If you can't get her going, then just get in and get out.*

Five gods. This was wrong. This was so many kinds of *wrong*—

"On your back," Orra said. "Shenni, you too."

Sweating and slightly horrified, Quinn anxiously lay back. He was stiff everywhere but the place where it mattered, and it seemed like Shenni felt the same way.

"Look at each other," Orra demanded. He felt her breath on his thigh. He turned his head, not expecting Shenni to obey as well, but she did.

"Hold her hand, *gentleman,*" Orra growled.

Gracelessly he fumbled for one of Shenni's hands. She allowed him to hold it. They stared at each other. She had dark brown eyes that made him think of mulched wood, or of truffles.

"Hi," he finally told her.

He had only an instant to appreciate Shenni's fleeting, rare smile before something hot and wet took hold of his penis. He winced and glanced down to see Orra's lips stretching as she hauled her mouth up his shaft. It was so sudden, it barely felt good.

Shenni's hand tensed in his, and he looked up at her. Her eyes were on Orra. She was angry.

"I'm sorry," he said. "I didn't have a choice...."

She glared at him. "Yeah, right."

He tried hard to think. Tried to fight the erection. "Jorr—Jorr made me," he said, fully aware of how pathetic he sounded.

"Ha. Really? You and I have that in common." She didn't sound as if she believed him, and he blinked a few times, attempting to separate part of his mind from the wet roving mouth running laps on his penis.

But then she blinked too, in surprise, and he knew without looking that Orra was touching her. Their fingers loosened as, if only for a moment, they both lost themselves in their own personal pleasures. Eyes closed, he listened to her breaths as they sped up, as *Orra* sped up, *five gods, dammit,* he was going to snap. He flung his eyes open and looked at her, her eyes were hooded and lost and he focused there, trying not to think about the unsightly sounds Orra was making, trying not to come where he wasn't supposed to, trying, trying, trying....

He watched a tear trickle down her cheek, her teeth bared in pleasure, her body rocking from what could *not* be gentle thrusts. She moaned, so softly he barely heard it beneath the wet sounds between them. He squeezed her hand, and she squeezed back and looked at him.

"I'm going to come," she breathed.

"Me too," he admitted.

She laughed hoarsely. "This is messed up...."

On a whim, Quinn leaned closer, kissing her on the mouth, forcing Orra's dreadlocks to tangle between their hips and legs. To his surprise, Shenni kissed him back, let go of his hand, and gripped his hip.

He responded by running his hand down her ribs and back up, smoothing his palms over her small breasts before tangling his fingers in her thin yellow braids. Her skin was darker than his—the skin of an Optic. He'd never touched an Optic like this....

Orra abruptly freed him of her lips, grabbed his hips and hauled him sideways, above Shenni. He fell into the position on instinct, his penis between her spread legs, his head already quivering against her wet flesh. He was close to the edge, aching; her knees closed on his hips as Orra lay beside Shenni and reached low with her fingers.

Shenni's neck strained as Orra played with her clitoris. Quinn's arms were starting to shake from holding him up. His ass felt poised and exposed, the sweat growing cold there.

"Stay where you are," Orra ordered him. "Go when she tells you."

He nodded, not even daring to try to touch himself for fear of coming all over her. He *had* to do this, had to keep his focus. *Get in, get out, and the Contract is sealed.* That's all she needed from him.

I'm just here to help, he told himself. *She'll die if she doesn't close a Rose Contract. If you can't close the contract....*

Shenni moaned beneath him, and though he wasn't inside her, he could feel enough flesh to know she was tensing. She twisted in pleasure as he raked her with his gaze. So small, so thin, *a virgin,* so close. Would she be tight? Would she... bleed?

It was the first time he'd thought this, and for an instant his erection went slack. The fog cleared; he could *hurt* this woman. She didn't want him—she wanted *Orra....*

"Oh... Seeing... Queen," she moaned, and with each word, her back arched higher, her legs spread wider, her sex pressed closer to his....

"Shenni," he begged her.

"I consent," she wept.

"Gentle," Orra warned, but he was already pushing, a slow walk from air into liquid. He shuddered as her walls closed around him, as her vagina squeezed like a dexterous fist. One of his hands gripped her braids as he came to a stop. He hadn't felt any resistance, no breaking flesh, just need and need and need—

Orra did something with her hand, and Shenni's legs snapped against his hip bones and she pulled his face to her neck as she cried out, the pulse between them going stiffer and angrier and her body shaking and—

"Gods *damn*," he breathed out, meeting her orgasm with his own. He tried to pull away, but she clung to him.

"Don't—please—stay—"

Orra laughed beside them. "I told you it would feel good."

One thrust. One. He was terrible. *Get in, get out,* indeed.

He felt each contraction as he emptied into her body. As all his energy flowed into hers.

An instant before he was too soft for comfort, Orra patted his back. "You can come out now," she said, nearly laughing.

"Don't wanna," he said, a bit unwisely. But something inside him had reverted to a child.

"But I have to lick you clean," Orra pouted.

He blinked at this, dazed, and finally extracted himself. He lay beside Shenni. Her hand found his.

"Thanks," she said, as Orra started to nuzzle his penis.

Quinn watched the ceiling spin. "For what?"

"It felt good," she said, "and you were nice to me. I'm glad it was you. That's all."

He wanted to ask her if there might be a second time, but he was almost certain she'd say no, so he shifted his attention downward. Orra wasn't having any luck getting him hard, but he appreciated the effort. He reached down and tugged on her, and she rose and lay next to him, one beautiful woman to both sides.

"I need time," he admitted. "I'm not a machine...."

Shenni slung her chest across his, and Orra did the same.

"That's okay," Orra said.

"*We* don't need time," Shenni added.

And Quinn closed his eyes, and *absolutely* did not sleep. It was the best contract that he'd ever signed.

EIGHT

NEITHER DOES FATE

Triggers: MF, first time.
Companion Books: Various.
Spoilers: None.

King Daisuke of Optic thought he was seeing things. The entire valley below him was *blue*.

"Quite fantastical, isn't it?" asked his tax adviser, Toru. "You can see why the taxes need raising."

Daisuke made a noncommittal noise in his throat. Only Toru would look at a valley blanketed by blue-leafed trees and think, *We ought to tax this place more.*

He nodded at the great black stone cavern, several stories high, out of which a string of carts and villagers was emerging. "And that's the source of the pyracite, I presume?"

"Precisely," Toru replied. "Apparently there was some kind of cave-in centuries ago, which hid the entrance from view. I'm told the villagers have been planning to live there—it has plenty of rooms carved into it. They believe it's the ancient underground palace of Eidan Tinker himself." Toru grinned. "Imagine how much the Audits would pay to vacation there."

Daisuke could practically see the silver dancing in the man's eyes. He shook his head and mounted his horse in a single movement. Might as well get this commandeering over with. The villagers weren't going to like it when he took over their mine.

As soon as Daisuke mounted, Toru twisted around to wave at the entourage of wagons and soldiers behind them. In response, men cantered forward to surround him. People shouted orders this way and that, and the wagon wheels turned again, bringing their little caravan down the dirt road. It was still rarely traveled, even after two full growing seasons of this valley's strange apples. If the villagers hadn't started selling blue cider to the villagers south of them, it might have been years yet before their treasure trove was discovered.

He was halfway to the cluster of wood huts bordering the orchard when a creature rode out of the rows of trees. It was a cragdeer, lithe and long-limbed, with black antlers as tall as a hedge. But unlike the wild cragdeer he normally glimpsed on the jagged outcrops of these northern mountains, this one was loping directly toward him, and it was alone.

"Would you look at that rack," Toru said. He turned to one of his own attendants. "Find a crossbowman and have him shoot that thing, will you?"

"Wait," Daisuke said, squinting in the failing light. There was something odd about the cragdeer. It ran too straight, and the shape—as if something *rose* it—

"It has a *rider*," he said, and awe swept over him yet again as the cragdeer drew nearer. Behind it, several more of the creatures bounded from the blue wood, all of them with their own riders.

"Impossible," Toru said. "No one can train cragdeer."

Daisuke wondered how long it would take for Toru to monetize the deer, too. He held out a hand to slow his entourage and signaled his guards to step back, before trotting forward to meet the first rider. He recognized her quickly as a woman, given the trailing length of her gray hair and the thinness of her waist. She pulled up short, turning the deer to the side with a harness. He was floored to see the reins were attached to the creature's antlers, not its snout.

And then he raised his gaze to the woman, and his heartbeat forgot itself. It took him several moments to breathe, and by that time her three fellow villagers had joined her. These were men, with younger mounts whose antlers were smaller. They scowled at Daisuke.

But the woman smiled.

"King Daisuke, I presume?" said the woman.

Beside him, Toru stiffened and opened his mouth. Daisuke raised a hand again, and Toru fell quiet.

The woman glanced between them. "Am I supposed to bow? You'll have to forgive me. I've been a long time out of polite society."

"There's no need for bowing," Daisuke said. "Yes, I am the king."

One of the male villagers spoke up. "And I suppose you'll be here to commandeer our mine, then? Or will it be taxes? Or goods?"

This time it was the woman who held up a hand for silence. She turned back to her men without losing her smile.

"Now, now, we'll have none of that," she said. "Let's wait to hear what the king has to say before we start dressing him down, shall we?" She gave a stiff nod to the man who had spoken. "Sasuke, please go down to the village and start the women cooking. These men will be wanting a good meal."

His scowl only slightly lessened, the man nodded shortly. "Yes, milady," he said, before urging his mount away.

The woman turned back, and Daisuke caught himself watching the way her hair dipped over her shoulder as she did so. "My apologies," the woman said. "I told the people here that this day would come, but of course, they are possessive of their home."

"You say that like you are not one of them," Daisuke replied. Her man had called her *milady*. "What is your name and rank?"

"Oh, no rank. I'm just a wandering cartographer. Yuki Barren, at your service." She bowed her head.

For a woman with no magic, nor any rank, she certainly seemed to be well-respected by these people. At this thought, Daisuke felt a flare of envy, but it passed. Envy was one of his father's worst habits, and he found it exhausting no matter who felt it.

"We appreciate your hospitality, Miss Yuki," Daisuke said. "I admit, I did not expect it."

"Naturally," she replied. Her smile was still in place, and yet it seemed genuine—although her canny gaze suggested he ought to tread carefully.

"You'll be wanting a tour of the orchard and the mine," she said, when he gave no response. "By the time we finish, the food should be ready." She angled her horse toward the trees, though she kept her eyes on his. He realized she's never once looked at Toru or the soldiers. Always at him.

His chest thudded. She *knew* she was beautiful. She was wielding that smile and that gaze like a weapon, and her long Optic hair had not been put up. It hung free, glinting silver, like the curving blade of a scythe; and the blue-on-blue of her dress clung to her slight frame in a way that made every curve sing.

He urged his horse to follow her without thinking, and only when he breached the edge of the orchard did he even notice that they weren't alone. While Yuki and her men were having no trouble navigating the orchard, Daisuke's soldiers crunched and tripped all around him. He heard swearing as they picked their way past the warren of low branches and crooked roots. Their horses had been trained for open-field combat, but these northern wilds were already proving too much for them. He caught Yuki smiling and his own lips pulled up at the silliness of the picture they must make.

Her cragdeer suddenly darted up next to him, and Yuki leaned close. "You think they'll drag the wagons in too?"

She said it with a laugh before loping forward again, so that his struggling guards didn't have to worry she might kill him. He chuckled to himself, and only when he heard the noise did he realize how foreign it sounded inside his own throat.

He signaled Toru. "Have the men set up in town. You and two guards can come with, on horse."

"But sire, only two—"

"I'll send my friends back," Yuki said, appearing behind Toru. The man jumped and turned to see her cocking her head. "Two guards can surely keep the king safe from one woman?" she asked, her eyes sparkling in the broken light of the canopy.

Toru grimaced, but in no time Daisuke had pulled up beside Yuki with only a few men to thud around behind him.

"I suppose you'll be wanting to know about the trees?" Yuki asked him, once he'd convinced Toru to hang back from the two of them.

Not really, he wanted to say. "I've never seen anything like them," he commented. "Are they a new cultivar of some kind?"

"Oh, no," she said. "They're a mountain breed. Very rare. I've been collecting seeds for ages, you see. These people were just the first to purchase them from me."

"So it was you who brought such wealth to them?" No wonder they treated her as they did.

She shrugged. "It seemed a shame not to grow the trees. And their village was subsisting off trapping—not my favorite practice. I figured I'd offer them another way out."

An animal lover, too? Perhaps that explained the cragdeer. "And the mine?" he asked. They were approaching it now, emerging from the edge of the orchard to stand before the great maw of the cavern.

"Oh, just a little something I discovered on accident," she said. "I led the villagers here for the valley, you see. For the trees. The soil here is very nutritious. And I found the cavern while hiking. Just knocked a stone free, and the rest came tumbling after."

"Ah. It would seem good fortune follows you."

She snorted. "Well, I *did* break my leg."

He laughed, which probably wasn't the most appropriate response, but she laughed too. He felt light, as if he were riding a cloud instead of a horse.

At the entrance to the mine, Yuki dismounted to disperse the villagers. When the place was emptied again, she led him into the darkness on foot. His companions all held a lantern, but no one handed one to Daisuke. His hands flexed from a strange nervousness as they proceeded into the cavern. The walls seemed to suck in the flamelight.

"The stone is called pyracite," Yuki said after Toru halted their whole group to look closer. "Otherwise known as dragon obsidian. You won't know of it, except from very old geological tomes, like those written by Eidan Tinker. It's actually a deep blue in the sunlight, not black."

"I remember reading of it," Daisuke said, because suddenly he did. In ages past, before his father had perished, he had once enjoyed chemistry. "If I remember correctly, it can be used to make magelights, though the process for that has been lost."

Yuki tilted her head at him. "Very good, my king." She said the words with a smile that upended his stomach.

"Come this way," she said. "I've something to show you."

He followed her like a loyal pet, growing more awake by the second. The nearer he came to her, the more intense her presence, as if the darkness made her more vibrant by comparison. He'd never been in love before, but he felt sure it began with this same overwhelming need to be near someone.

The passage thinned. Toru complained. The guards' armor clanked between the walls.

"I swear I'm not trying to kill you, or anything," Yuki said. "But there really is something spectacular just down this—"

Her words cut off with a grunt as Daisuke tripped on a stone and fell against her. Her lantern fell, and its flame went out.

"My—my king—"

"I'm sorry, sorry—"

They were close, chest-to-chest, and even she was flustered now, a thought which made his cheeks flame. But the passage was too thin, and he was having trouble righting himself. His knees clicked against wall whenever he tried to turn.

Her body was tense against his. "Please, Daisuke, I can't hold—"

And then Yuki's body caved in.

He realized too late that she had been holding him up, that she had stepped over some sort of incline just as he'd tripped. Now they both tumbled forward into the thin cavern. She cried out as the back of her head struck the ground, and he reached for her, but he was sliding now. The ground was loose gravel, and the flamelight was growing distant. Toru shouted after him.

The world started to rumble.

The ground shook around him, beneath him. A loud growl chased them down the tunnel. His hands scraped for purchase on the obsidian walls, but the glassy blue surface was far too smooth. Yuki was quiet, unconscious, and pulling away from him. He snatched for her so he wouldn't lose her.

Then they came to a stop, and the world fell still. Somewhere close by, he heard the trickling of water.

Someone shouted behind him, but it was muffled, sounding much more distant than it should have been. Dazed, Daisuke looked up the way they'd come. A tiny little speckle of light shone back that way, like a single mote of glowing dust.

Yuki groaned, and he turned his attention back to her. He felt her head, and sighed his relief; no blood.

"It's all right," he said. "We just fell a little ways." Turning back toward his men, he shouted that they were fine. There was no response. He tried again.

"They—they probably can't hear you," Yuki said, her voice gritted form pain. "I think there was a cave-in."

He looked back at the flicker of light again. It could easily be lantern light showing through a single tiny hole, with the rest of the light blocked by stone.

She laughed hoarsely and sat up, their legs touching. "My bad luck again. It never stops."

"You can't really think this was *your* fault?" he replied.

She rose to her hands and knees in the blackness. He couldn't see her, only feel her, as she felt around the area. His pulse quickened when her hair brushed his forearm.

"Looks like the entrance to the chamber collapsed," she said. "We're stuck, and it's a pretty tight space."

"Can they dig us out, you think?" he asked.

"Oh, sure. This actually happens a lot." Her voice turned back to him. "Dragon obsidian deteriorates, you see. Its strength came from the presence of dragons, but dragons have been gone for centuries. Now it's nearly as fragile as glass."

Her hand slipped into his. "See for yourself," she said,

placing something round in his palm. *Too* round, as if it were man-made.

"A magelight," she said. "It used to stand on a pedestal here. You can feel how it's cracking."

Indeed, he could feel it, a hairline starburst of cracks. He rubbed a thumb over it, considering.

"Do you have a light?" he asked. Her lantern was long gone. "A match, or something."

"Yes," she said. "Standard fare for a spelunker. But we'll need something to burn, and it might suck up our oxygen—"

"No, I just need the light, for just a moment. I want to try something."

A pause. He could practically feel her frowning. She shifted, her shoulder leaning against him. His body reacted to her presence, and the situation struck him hard. A beautiful woman, a tight space, and no one to watch them. Possibly hours before they would be freed.

She seemed to be having trouble getting into the pockets of her split skirts, so he held her arm. She slowed, her skin warm. She turned toward him. He could feel her breath on his mouth.

"I found it," she said softly. Her tone had changed.

He swallowed so loudly it might as well be a gulp. His own words were raw as he said, "Light it up." He forced his gaze down to the glass orb in his hand.

"Ready?" she whispered.

"Ready."

And he brought his magic up to the surface of his skin.

It was a relatively useless magic, especially for a king; most people believed him to be a Tinker mage when he wasn't. He took the name—his father's name—to hide his own weakness but in reality, he was only a Scan mage. While Tinker mages could directly affect objects, Scan mages could only *read* them. It was like reading thoughts, though objects had no thoughts. A better way to say it is that he read *memories*.

"Ready," he said, and Yuki lit the match. Daisuke looked deep into the stone. As a mage born in Optic, his magic connected through sight. He had to see an object to read it.

The cracked glass orb glittered up at him, its spidery white cracks catching flame. Its memories were of cool flame, of flickering, and of blue. And of a thousand utterances of a single word: *ahni*.

The flame went out, burning down, plunging them both into darkness. Daisuke focused on the feel of the orb in his palm.

"*Ahni*," he said.

And it lit.

The blue magelight was weak, its tendrils marred by its cracks. But whatever enchantment still dwelt inside it must still be intact.

"Amazing," Yuki exhaled, her dark eyes coruscating with blue flame. "How did you do that?" She met his eyes.

His throat tightened. His body heated. He was *reacting* to her. Under his trousers, he stirred, nearly insensate from her closeness.

"It's my magic," he exhaled. He tried to explain. But the word wouldn't come, and her eyes dipped to his mouth. Her chest rose and fell, a quick breath. Was she nervous? He didn't dare look at the edge of her neckline, where her dark skin met the pale trim. Didn't dare think of the flesh beneath it.

"Maybe," she said softly, before swallowing dryly. She shifted her body toward him. "Maybe this wasn't such bad luck after all...."

He set the magelight down. The cold flame kept burning.

"No one's coming for us for hours," she whispered.

Daisuke couldn't fathom how he'd gotten here, what

miracle had made this happen. But he didn't put his hands on her, didn't lean close. He knew he was a king, and that she was a commoner. If he made any move at all, it would be an order. *I am a king, and you will obey.* The power here had to be hers.

"My king," she said, then stopped, as if she meant to say more.

"Daisuke," he corrected her.

She was dead still. "Daisuke."

The word made the hair rise on his neck.

"I didn't expect you to be so handsome, Daisuke," she said.

Oh, five gods. Five gods, take me now.

"And I didn't expect to find a woman in charge of a mining town," he said. "I didn't expect a woman who could tame a cragdeer, who mapped the wilds for a living. Who's more loved by her people than I'll ever be."

She raised her hand to his cheek. He could barely contain himself. He leaned into her touch. He was *burning*.

"Is it just me," she said, "or does this feel fated?"

He closed his eyes. "Senseless take me. It does."

Yuki laughed. "Oh, *they* aren't the ones you should be worried about." Her hand slid down the back of his neck. He opened his eyes in time to see her closed eyes lean close. To feel her lips brushing soft against his.

He seized the arm she was using to hold herself up, and pulled her against him. She made a huffing sound against his mouth, her own lips parted. She looked down at him with glaze, flaming eyes.

Tension quivered between them, a precipice. She dropped them both of the edge by thrusting her mouth against his.

It was sudden and fierce, the way her tongue snaked past his teeth, the way she swung his whole body down with the force of the kiss. He lay on his back, aching but inundated, desire roiling through him as her chin knocked against his, as her grip on his hair turned to claws, as her other hand stretched its way down—

She gripped him through his clothing. Groaned into his mouth. He met the sound with a cry of his own. She tightened her hand on him again, then loosened, then tightened it, all while her tongue ran across his lower lip.

"Consent to me," she growled as his back arched to meet her strokes. He slapped both his hands to the tight walls to hold himself in his place.

He struggled to think. There was something he'd forgotten. A responsibility. Where had it gone?

"I consent to—to—"

"I want it all. Or I want nothing."

He groaned, his neck stretching as he looked away from her, barely able to see his own fingernails clutching at the stone wall. She had to know what she was asking, far removed from polite society or not. He was a noble, and nobles in Optic were celibate. Until marriage, he couldn't make love.

How had he forgotten that? Why hadn't he remembered this even once? What exactly had his plan been, if she decided to kiss him?

"I can—for you—"

Her hand clutched at him, then released. He yearned to have the touch back. But then she was tickling the hairs beneath his navel, deftly flipping his belt open, yanking the strings of his breeches.

Five gods, he hadn't expected to be *taken*. He was a king. Kings *took*.

"I won't tell anyone if you won't," she said, curling her fist around his bare skin. She stroked down, pulling the flesh so tight it hurt. He raised his knees in reaction, but the small pain made him crazy. After her knuckles met his balls, she let him go and raised a hand. She spat into her palm and went back to work.

"Women have done this for you before, right?" she asked as he slowly lost his mind. He nodded, kicking out, trying to hold himself tight to more walls. She retreated, her hands running down the backs of his knees. She ducked. "And have they done this?"

Her mouth sank onto his penis, and all the tightness went out of him. He gasped as pressure pulled him into her throat. Her muscles closed around him, her teeth rubbing, her tongue dancing up the looser flesh. She popped off, and then scooped up his balls with her tongue.

He arched his back again, surprised, his penis ramming her nose. She seized the chance to tug his trousers off him. His toes curled as she gripped him at the base of his penis, her hand like a vise and her mouth going fast. She sucked down on his head, the flesh flipping past her lips, the sounds she made so loud that surely Toru could hear them.

That thought sobered him—not much, but just barely enough to make him realize this was much too one-sided. He sank his fingers into her hair and pulled her off him, then clawed at the shoulders of her dress until she drew nearer.

"Is this what you want?" she said, her weight flattening him now. One of her hands inched up between them, and she pulled at her neckline. First one dark nipple, then the other, spilled out onto his chest. One of his hands fought for the split in her skirts.

She gasped as he found her wet and waiting. He sank two fingers into the giving flesh. He'd done this, too—he'd done all of this at least once—but never with the fervor that he felt beneath this woman now.

Yuki raised herself up and thrust against him, moaning as he swirled, his touch mapping the landscape inside her. The pads of his hands rubbed at the flesh outside of her vagina, covering the area where her clitoris must be hiding.

She turned them both sideways, curling one leg around his hip, her breasts close to his face now as she struggled to give him access. His own forearm rubbed his penis as he worked at her. Her body shook as he built her up.

This—all of this—he could do this. But sex was the property of his future wife. If he could just make her come, he could finish himself after. He could make it impossible for him to fail in his vows.

He told himself this, even as she shuddered and gripped him, her hands deep in his shoulder blades. He told himself this as her orgasm tightened on his fingers. As he took his hand away and started touching himself.

But his hands were wet now, wet with her body. He stroked himself closer and closer to her heat. She helped him, hips swinging forward. When she caught his head between her swollen lips, he groaned and let himself go.

No sex. No sex.

He gripped her butt. She thrust down with a cry.

He shuddered and stilled. They both did. His breaths came fast. He pulled her forehead to his. Their noses touched, their mouths hot between them.

He'd broken his vow, and he didn't care.

She held his shoulder for leverage, and rolled against him, his penis sinking deep with her movement. Her flesh clung to him, hotter and tighter than her mouth had. He craved to see how far this tunnel went.

"Is this all right?" she whispered, knowing what she had done.

He knew he's asked for it. "Yes."

"Where—do you want me?" she asked, before kissing him.

He answered by flipping on top of her.

Yuki's legs widened, and she fumbled with her skirts until he had a clear path into her body. He took a moment to suckle just one of her breasts. But it made his penis jerk—her nipples were dangerous.

He stretched out, and his penis slunk into her. "I don't have any orchid," she whispered into his neck.

He nodded against her hair and thrust anyway. He'd be careful. He had *better* be careful.

Bracing himself on his arms, he fell into a rhythm. She held his quivering biceps and met every beat. They were one single wild thing in this forgotten place. It was a dream. It couldn't be real.

Her heavy breathing turned to cries. She thrust harder against him. Every time he breathed out, it was a desperate grunt. They made animal sounds and animal movements as the ache of his pleasure surged nearer.

Then her walls tightened, clutching at him. Her thighs closed against his hips. The wetness, the heat, it changed the gravity in his head. Everything flipped, and he started to come.

He cried out and yanked out of her, caught by surprise as it happened. He spilled himself all over her skirts. His face dropped to her stomach as the pulsing rippled through him. She toyed with his hair and whispered his name.

His arms were dead and shaky as he lowered himself, nuzzling the fabric aside to put his mouth on her. He had to rest his cheek on her inner thigh, unable to hold himself up, but he could still part her lips and search with his tongue.

As the last spurt left his body, he found what he wanted, and sucked. While his bare penis collapsed to the cold stone, he pressed his palms to her hips. One palm was still slick with his own release.

"A... Again?" she whispered. He nodded, his nose brushing hair.

She sighed and relaxed into heavy silence. He licked and he pressed and he pulled.

After six mind-numbing minutes, her hips kicked up, her thighs snapping to his head tight enough to make him let go. But he didn't want it over, she he dropped three fingers inside her, to give her orgasm something to grip.

He breathed into her navel until it was over, until the only sounds were the distant water and breathing. With weak fingers she guided him up to her, until they lay side by side in the ethereal light.

"I'm sorry," she said. "I just ruined you, didn't I?"

He shook his head and kissed her. "Come with me," he said.

She leaned away from him, her eyes a deep blue from the firelight. "Come with you? Where?"

"Home," he said. "To the capital. I want you to teach me how you do it."

Yuki frowned, and the look melted him all over again. He couldn't believe he held something so perfect inside his pitiful arms.

"Do what, exactly?" she asked.

"Make them love you. Your people."

She smiled with one side of her mouth. "I didn't *make* anyone love me."

Seemed to work on me, he thought.

"My father died before he was supposed to," Daisuke said, "and I have no idea what I'm doing. My father was a brutal king, and most people hated him. I don't want to be that—but I don't want to be weak.

"So come with me. Help me. Show me how to command. I can see in these people's eyes how they love you. But they also listen. They *want* to listen.

"Please, Yuki. I need someone like you."

She stared at him, her eyes darting just slightly as she

peered between both of his eyes. His chest felt light in that gaze, in the presence of her. He understood he was madly in love.

"I'm just a cartographer, Daisuke," she said. She ran a hand down his arm and back up. "This—this was wonderful. But there will be rumors. If this happens again—"

"Your village keeps the mines," he blurted. "And they pay no taxes. Name your salary, Yuki. I need you."

She laughed at that, and nothing else mattered. His broken vows, his angry citizens, the thousand pressures of a kingdom—all he could think of was her.

"Well, all right then," she said. "But as your new adviser, I highly suggest you tax them *something*. Otherwise they'll forget you exist."

He nodded and pulled her closer. "You make a fair point." A scraping noise sounded back the way they had fallen.

Yuki glanced at the lantern light now pouring through the fallen stone. "Oh, dear, it seems our alone time has run out."

He sighed and said, "Duty waits for no man."

Her eyes gleamed in the magelight as she faced him again. She pressed her nose to his and said, "Neither does fate."

NINE

SLEIGHT OF HAND

TRIGGERS: MM, CASUAL ENCOUNTER, SUBMISSION, ADULTERY.
COMPANION BOOK: BRING ME DOWN.
SPOILERS: NONE.

Captain Ichigo Obey was balls-deep in a card game when he first met Tanaka Barren. The kid caught his eye because he was failing spectacularly to break through the crowd that surrounded the makeshift playing table.

"Excuse me—I need to—*excuse—*"

Ichigo grinned in a half-smile, watching the poor kid impale himself on shoulders and elbows and the handles of swords jutting out from the other soldier's hips. The young soldier grunted and declared that he needed to pass with endless politeness, unlike the men all around him, who were tossing coins on the upturned haycart and swearing colorfully.

"You gonna guess or not?" Ichigo's opponent asked, and Ichigo raised his eyebrows and turned his attention back to the game.

"Oh, is it that time already?" he said lackadaisically, as if he'd forgotten the rules of Kill the Coward.

"Don't stall," his opponent sneered. "Or I'll take your bet up front next time."

"And I'll take yours up the back," Ichigo responded, and a wave of amused *whoo-hoo-hooo*s swept the crowd. Grinning at his opponents disgusted expression, he patted the Coward card and said, "I call the Two of Fingers. Which coincidentally will *also* be a part of my payment."

The crowd went wild, laughing and punching each other on the shoulders and inadvertently making way for the harried little soldier to fumble through. He landed beside Ichigo's opponent with a surprised gasp, spreading the cards around. His opponent swore and shot to his feet, gripping the boy by the collar.

"What are you playing at, mutt?" the man roared, using the slang term for a rankless newbie.

Ichigo also stood. "Now, now, Jiro. No need to make a scene. If you don't want to suck my cock, you can just say so."

Jiro's cheeks reddened so much that his skin turned maroon. He shook the boy and said, "You did this! You hired him to muss the cards."

Ichigo pursed his lips and nodded, as if to say, *Ah, yes, it does look suspicious, doesn't it?* Now that the kid had mussed up the cards, there was no way to tell for sure which card had been the Coward.

"Well," he said, "there is one way." He held out a palm. "Flip them all."

Jiro didn't seem to understand, which only made him angrier. He shoved the kid away, where the poor mutt stumbled again when none of his fellows moved to help him.

Jiro flipped all the cards in front of him—which included

his own face-down hand and the few remaining cards in the unflipped deck. He frowned.

"It's not here."

"You mean the Two of Fingers?" Ichigo said. "How unfortunate. If it's nowhere in the pile, then it must never have been there at all. Therefore, I must have guessed wrong."

Jiro brightened. Smiled darkly. "I win, then."

Ichigo slipped the Two of Fingers from his sleeve into his back pocket. "Yes, it seems you do."

TANAKA FOLLOWED ICHIGO, as did half the retinue from the bar—a poor word to describe an upturned haycart and a stolen keg of ale, but suitable nonetheless. The moon, almost full, lit the soldier's camp all around them, lighting up a forest as thick as brick walls. They were guarding the Soma/Optic border, but they were nowhere special. The men were all antsy to go to the front lines, where the action was. Ichigo preferred to find his action right here.

"Sir," Tanaka called. "Sir—Sir—"

Ichigo was following Jiro to the man's tent. "You're Tanaka Barren," he said, without meeting the boy's eyes. "My new page."

"Sir, yes, sir."

Ichigo cocked an eyebrow at the kid. Green as they come. It was clear on his face that it was only just now dawning on him where Ichigo was headed, and what he was about to do.

"Major said he'd rein me in somehow," Ichigo said, stepping over a heap of horse manure. "Sadly, you've already failed."

"But sir," Tanaka said, his voice lowering so as not to be heard by the jeering crowd a few paces behind them, "you guessed right, sir. I saw you palm the Coward card."

Ichigo was impressed. After casually pushing aside a drunken soldier who wandered into his path, he said, "But you can't know I guessed *right*."

"Um. But I can, sir." Tanaka sheepishly held up the Two of Fingers card. Ichigo actually missed a step, and stopped just short of patting his back pocket to check for it. He didn't need the other men to get the idea he'd been cheating.

Tanaka hastily secreted the card inside the collar of his brigandine, shoving inside a bit of cheap chain mail to do it. "You could have won, sir. I messed it up—"

"Ah," Ichigo interrupted, "Here we are." They had just arrived at a darkened tent that everyone knew belonged to Jiro, however much the man preferred them to believe otherwise. "Wait here for me, will you? I shouldn't be long."

With that, he ducked into the tent. Silence and darkness befell him, and he began to take off his armor and leather guards and then finally his tunic and breeches as he waited for Jiro to return. The man would be taking a few more shots of liquor, as Ichigo's first-time lovers usually did. There had been enough of them now that the other soldiers merely laughed at them as they made their walks of shame to his tent. In reality, many of the others were secretly jealous. Most of them felt that, in the dark, *anything* was better than nothing at all—and it had been weeks since these men had met a woman.

Ichigo, however, had his pick of the litter. And his pick for the night had been Jiro.

A whipping of fabric, a few grassy steps. "Where are you, pretty-boy?" Jiro groused.

Ichigo reached for him and caught his swaying elbow. He didn't say anything. He'd lost the right to speak or even to decide his own actions for the next few minutes. All the better to Jiro to enact whatever fantasy pleased him—to imagine Ichigo was a woman, perhaps.

The man stopped in place, turning toward Ichigo and reaching out a hand. He touched bare flesh on Ichigo's pectoral muscle, and the charge or arousal made the air fat between them. Jiro's rough palms rounded Ichigo's ribs and then splayed against his back and pushed him forward. His breaths were heavy in the darkness, the edges sanded down. With insistent pressure he forced Ichigo onto his cot, and Ichigo bent over obediently. He was hard, and while he waited for the other man to finish taking off all the leather and steel that came between them, Ichigo pumped himself a few times for good measure.

"Will it... will it be wet enough?" Jiro said roughly—timidly, even. Like most of them, he wasn't sure how this worked. He only knew that he wanted it, that he needed release after weeks or even months with no friend but his hand.

Ichigo slipped back off the cot, turned, and knelt. He found Jiro's penis with both hands and pulled it into his mouth.

Jiro jerked at first, but there was no one to watch him or judge him, and he melted into the darkness as Ichigo pulled his tight flesh past his teeth. Ichigo's mouth could have belonged to anyone, and Jiro was soon wracked with hot sighs and unashamed shudders. Ichigo groaned in his throat as he pulled Jiro as far down as he could, which wasn't enough, not really. His lips couldn't even reach the base of Jiro's cock.

This was the reason he'd lost.

He pulled away, the inside of his lips soft and wet against the man's bulging head. With a subtle smack, he freed the man from the warm haven of his mouth and said, "Is that wet enough for you?"

Jiro murmured something, and gripped Ichigo by the shoulders and spun him back around. He thrust and missed, swore, and repositioned himself with his hand. Ichigo's pulse was a war drum as hard flesh split his cheeks, nuzzling past the tickling hairs. He'd waited all night for this, knowing it was coming. His own penis twitched, ready to expend itself. With a penis that large, it shouldn't take long—

His lover pushed, growled, and pushed harder. Ichigo drew a breath, sharp and ending in a cry he barely stifled. His penis did a weird double-jump, his balls swaying in the cool autumn air. Still Jiro went deeper, forcing his way past the tight ring and into the giving flesh beyond.

Already the pleasure was expanding inside Ichigo. Sometimes, the right size and shape nudged him just right. He gripped himself with one hand and balanced himself precariously with the other, his biceps clenching from effort. He growled as Jiro's cock tunneled back out of him and back in again, as his body provided its own form of lubricant while keeping him just dry enough to feel all the sensation.

"Oh, gods," Jiro cursed, as if he were angry, and he shoved forward and back out before Ichigo could recapture his breath. Within seconds, the two were rocking in a frenetic pace, Ichigo already sweating with the effort to keep from flopping over. He could barely stroke himself, only hold on for dear life as the other man expended all the energy he'd been saving up for a wife or lover or prostitute back home. This wasn't sex, Jiro would tell himself later. It wasn't any kind of adultery.

But Ichigo knew the truth. He was a toy, a sin, a temptation. If he'd been a top, it wouldn't have worked, but he preferred this. He preferred the power and energy of others to pour into him. All he had to do was stay upright and feel the pleasure swell from his ass to his balls to his stomach, chest, arms, fingers, toes—every part of him quivering with sensation he could never achieve on his own. He'd learned to cheat at cards just to give men the excuse to win. He wanted them. He wanted *all of them*.

Jiro spread him wide, grunting now, audible to anyone who

might be listening, and they likely were. Get enough men together and drunk enough and they could become a little bit curious, a little bit depraved. He let Jiro shove every inch of that curiosity into him, let him groan his depravity against Ichigo's bare back, his cheek against Ichigo's flesh, his wet lips spread open and trailing saliva as he lost all control and started fucking to come. Ichigo felt the change as the man pulsed inside him, his balls whipping between Ichigo's cheeks and leaving sweat behind. He smelled dirt and, inexplicably, sandalwood as he finally squeezed his own penis, pumped once, and put both hands down to hold his rear end high and ready.

Their breathing tangled, a furious back-and-forth of exhalations, and Jiro pulled clear out of him and slammed back in, the flesh making way, Ichigo's back arching as he threw his head back—

Ichigo gritted his teeth and cried out between them, sounding like a man with a gag. His penis surged upright and some of his ejaculate raked across his wrist. His whole body tingled until he felt he was floating, rocking on a wild sea in a slow-moving dream. Jiro gripped his shoulders, digging his jagged fingernails into Ichigo's flesh as he kept ramming, kept spreading, until—

Ichigo slumped forward, folding the spare blanket aside to cover his cum as the other man sprawled atop him, practically convulsing from pleasure as he spent himself. Ichigo would be draining hot fluid for hours, but it was worth it. Always worth it.

He knew the drill, though. No words. No more touching. As soon as Jiro pulled out and rolled over to gasp quietly to himself, Ichigo stood and dressed. It took a long time, in the pure dark, with nothing but the faintest firelight through the tent walls to guide him. He watched Jiro as the man turned into a silhouette, large and muscular with his fat cock curling sadly against him. The rumors hadn't been wrong, and Ichigo had enjoyed himself. There might even be a second time, or a third.

"You ever want to play cards again," he said, "you just say the word."

And then he was gone.

TANAKA WAITED OUTSIDE, as pale as a pecan, his eyes giving away their hazel tints in the moonbeams.

"Ah," Ichigo said, "you're a trooper for waiting."

Tanaka swallowed dryly, as if trying to figure out what to say. "You lost on purpose," he rasped.

"I would think that was obvious."

Tanaka stared at him, then past him, into the line of black between the tent flaps. He seemed to be realizing that the task of "reining in" his new master was going to be much more impossible than he had first thought.

"Does... does everyone know that you're... like that?" he breathed.

"Like what? Gay as a daisy?"

The kid swallowed. "Yes."

Ichigo grinned and was about to respond, when he narrowed his eyes instead, looking closer. There was something on this kid's face, something he recognized distantly. He'd seen it on himself almost a decade before, in his first lover's bathroom mirror.

"I'll be damned," he said. "You're one of us."

The kid warmed the air with his blushing, and it took him a few moments to find his voice. "I—I don't know sir," he said.

"You are." Ichigo leaned closer. "Oh, gods. You're only just now realizing, aren't you? Connecting the dots?" He shook his head and straightened, throwing his chain mail—which he'd never fully reattached—over his shoulder like a towel. Shrugging with that same shoulder, he indicated that Tanaka should follow him, and they began to walk back to Ichigo's tent. Tanaka said nothing. He just processed.

"No wonder you learned to pickpocket," Ichigo said softly. There were no other soldiers in this sleepy side of camp, all of them having wandered off when Ichigo had taken too long to emerge from Jiro's tent. They waited, sometimes, to see if his lovers were too quick, just so they had reason to mock them. He'd made many men targets in this way, but it wasn't until this moment, walking through the dozing camp with a boy who'd only just realized his sexuality, that Ichigo found himself feeling bad for his actions.

"I don't know what you mean, sir," Tanaka said.

Ichigo rolled a hand, distracted

"You know. Getting close to people. Sticking your fingers where they didn't belong. How much of the thrill was from the theft, and how much from the closeness, do you think?"

And why this sudden onslaught of guilt? Why am I just now growing a conscience?

Perhaps it was the honesty of the thing. The bare look on the kid's face in the instants before he stopped and spread a hand across his nose and cheeks, as if with that simple act, he could blot out the truth.

"Hey, now," Ichigo said, stopping and putting a hand on Tanaka's shoulder. "It's not all bad."

"My father... my father will... he'll...."

"Shh, shh," Ichigo said, gently wheeling the kid in the right direction. He couldn't imagine what it had been like, all those years of loneliness, with a family that bore down on his feelings with hate. Ichigo's own family couldn't have cared less about him, straight or not. Regardless, most of the men in this camp couldn't go a month without lovemaking of whatever kind they could manage. But this kid had never made love at all. Had probably been too afraid to.

They stepped into Ichigo's tent, where Ichigo was quick to light his oil lamp to put the kid at ease, to let him know Ichigo wasn't going to try anything with him.

"Sit," he said, indicating his cot. Tanaka didn't move at first, but Ichigo didn't press as he removed his brigandine and most of his armor. He kept all his underleathers securely intact, and then sat cross-legged on the bare dirt, expectant.

Finally, Tanaka did sit, right on the edge of the cot. His eyes were red-rimmed from unspent tears.

"Go on," Ichigo said. "You must have questions."

Tanaka closed his eyes, drew a breath—and he asked.

TEN

THE POISONER OF CORINTH

Triggers: MF, adultery, substance use, unhealthy
obsession, BDSM.
Companion Book: First of Her Kind.
Spoilers: Slight.

The poisoner lived a shady and humble life, in a shady
and humble part of town. Here in this far corner of
Corinth, the people meandered the gray streets by day, but
walked with silent purpose at night. The pall of dangerous
magic clung to every new stone and brick, and no one dared to
test it. Swords never clashed in these alleyways.

There were more silent ways to kill.

The poisoner's shop knelt at the center of the district like a
man with his hands on a grave. Squat and roofed in glittering
glass, the building was overgrown with vines despite being
three years new, and it saw a steady stream of business at all
hours of the day.

Today, however, the poisoner tapped his sales counter,
alone in the shop with his thoughts. As one of the only mages in

history to be bestowed by a dragon, he was closer to magic than most. And he could feel something now which the second generation could not.

Something in the world was amiss.

The cheerful bell over the shop door tinkled, and his wife Sumi stepped through. "I've brought some ham," she said, stepping up to his counter. "How are things today?"

"Slow," he said, distracted, not hungry. But he took his lunch from her hands and gave her his thanks, landing a fond kiss on her forehead.

As he unwrapped the package, Sumi rubbed her bulging stomach; their third child was now well on the way. "I've heard news out of Doraegon," she said. "They say Zandaka has torn his hoard apart. His seekers have all fled in fear."

The poisoner snorted. "Did his last Tribute turn his stomach?" He had eaten the humans only his month. All of the dragons had.

"I'm serious, Lotan," Sumi said. "People are afraid that the war has come back. That the dragons are rampaging again."

"Every time a dragon farts, people say that," said the poisoner, though a stone of unease had already formed in his gut. Still, he leaned forward and patted her hand. "Go back home, Su. You need to rest. I'll be there soon if things don't pick up."

His wife smiled at him in that bright way she had, like he was a wise teacher who'd praised her. Love swelled in his chest, a rare feeling. Of all the women he had chased in his life, she was the only one who'd made him feel this.

"Very well," she said, kissing him chastely over the counter. He watched her wobble and sway out the door, already growing bored in her absence. He should be working, but after that news, he'd never keep his mind on the task.

Suddenly he felt sick, intensely sick. The rows of shelving

in the shop seemed to melt. The multicolored glass vials, the overgrown potted plants, and the thick dusty sunlight swirled around him. But the episode ended quickly, leaving him gasping for breath, like a dry rag wrung for its very last drop.

Immediately he thought he'd been poisoned or enchanted. He turned to his lunch first, but the package of ham lay unopened. He thought of Sumi's kiss—

No. She would never hurt me.

"My, my, don't you look pale," said a voice, and he started. A cloaked woman stood behind a row of his shelves, peering at him through one of the bottles. When had she entered? He didn't remember. His mind was trapped in a cloud.

"Oh, don't hurt yourself by thinking so hard," said the woman. "The feeling will pass in a minute."

Her voice was rough, but not from age. So she had been the one to enchant him.

Anger gripping his chest, the poisoner leaned under the counter and pulled out a dagger. He stabbed its tip into the wooden counter, a warning. The knife was poisoned the full length of its blade.

"I don't take kindly to troublemakers," he said. "State your business, mage."

He couldn't see the woman's eyes under the lip of her hood, but he could see the smile as she prowled behind the bottles, emerging from the aisle to face him.

"Something tells me you'll take kindly to this troublemaker," she said. Her chin rose. "Was that your wife?"

The rage flared inside him. "Is that a threat?"

"No. An observation. But she's quite homely, don't you think? Though I suppose you never did care for looks, so long as the parts were intact."

The poisoner snatched up his blade and rounded the counter. "Why, you—"

Dizziness. Haziness. Pain.

He was gasping again, this time on the floor, the woman standing over him with his knife in her hands. He watched her survey the blade, unable to gather himself. Then she tossed the blade aside with a thunk.

"Really, Lotan?" she said. "You're dealing in poisons? When there is so much *more* you could do?"

There was something in her voice that he didn't like—something he had seen a few times before. It was the sound of pure hatred, barely contained.

This person had come here for vengeance.

"Get... out," he exhaled, reaching for the bottom of the nearest shelf. He could see one of the emergency poisons he had secreted there, for situations exactly like this.

She stepped on his wrist, not hard, but enough. "Oh, Lotan," she said, "you never were one to give up, but you really must pay more attention. Do you think me the sister of one of your victims? The mother of someone dead to your art?"

She laughed, a rocky and imbalanced sound. It drew his gaze up to her face, to the silver hair in her hood—

And all at once, he knew who she was.

The woman saw him stiffen, and she grinned down at his face, her cobalt eyes made black by shadow. She took her foot off him wrist and held her hand out to him.

He had read a story once, about a man fleeing trouble. The book had proclaimed the man's pulse to be so strong in his ears that the man could not hear his own thoughts.

It had always seemed like pretty words to the poisoner. But as he took the woman's hand, he met that same sensation, his pulse a new voice in his head.

She led him back to the counter, where he leaned against it for balance. Staring, helpless, as the woman's fingernails traced his jawline, as a thousand long-dead needs and emotions came flaring back to life.

"So, you remember me, *Lotan.*"

He nodded, barely able to hear her. He swallowed. It was like eating sand.

The woman thumbed his lips, her eyes tracing them hungrily. "Lotan Form. What an impressive name. Does your wife know it's not the one you were born with? That you chose it to start a new life for yourself, a life you could bear to face without *me?*"

The poisoner wanted to cry, to collapse, to kiss her. *Sumi. Think of Sumi....*

The woman dropped her hand to her collar, pulling her cloak aside slowly. His gaze locked on her dark, sultry fingers.

"I have a proposition for you," said the woman, as her cleavage came into view. "A *partnership*, so to speak."

The poisoner tried and failed to remember his wife, the way she looked with his firstborn in her arms. It had been seven years since he'd last felt this power, but the craving returned now as if it had never been gone, and Sumi was lost to the tides of his need.

"What do you want?" the poisoner croaked, his breeches going tighter each second. He couldn't look away from the crack between her perfect breasts. He wanted to see so much *more.*

"I need you to make something for me," said the woman, leaning closer, her fingers playing at the neckline of her dress. "Something that will make us a fortune."

The poisoner reached out to touch her, to make sure she was real.

"Tell me what I need to do."

✤

FOR WEEKS after that first encounter, the poisoner existed in frenzy. He woke early, stayed late, and kept the store closed. He made love to his wife every night that she let him.

For her part, Sumi seemed to enjoy it. His desire kept her flushed. She felt so *desirable*. Her husband wanted her, no matter her size.

But she didn't know how many times he used his own hands, when she wasn't there for the taking. For seven years of his life, he'd fought down this obsession, but he let it back in like the addiction it was. He'd told himself so many times that it was over.

Now he knew it had only begun.

But as time wore on and his third child was born, the poisoner began to have second thoughts. After all, he *did* love his wife, even if it was a much saner love. Sumi had saved him from himself, pulled him up from the booze, given him a family and a home and a purpose. He owed her his loyalty more than anything.

And so, on the second month, he made his decision. He would finally choose to do what was right.

⊕

THE WOMAN RETURNED with the same haze as before, warping the whole room around her.

She caught him while he was restocking his tonics. Suddenly appearing behind him, she gripped his shoulders to steady him. Her breath tickled the hairs near his ear.

"Do you have what I want?" she asked him.

His pulse slammed his skin, racing down to his crotch.

"Yes. I have it," he breathed.

She let him fetch her prize, her dark gaze possessive, her

lips curled into a knowing smile. He scurried into his back hall and returned with her order.

Its beauty paled in the shadow of *her*.

The woman fingered the petals of his masterpiece. Once blue, the orchid had turned black with poison. He explained to her how it worked.

"And nullbands won't stop it?" she said, marveling.

"No. I found a bypass for that."

She smiled softly at him. Her palm drifted to his cheek. "You're a genius, Master Form."

He grinned foolishly, his body alive with the praise, with the title he had never heard from her lips. "And you're as stunning as you ever were," he told her. He couldn't help himself.

"Always the flatterer," she said, placing the potted plant on the counter. With a casual shrug, she flipped back her cloak. The fabric fell away from her face and off her bare shoulders. "The seven years haven't aged me?" she asked.

"Not at all," he insisted, not seeing the new lines, completely missing the shadows under her eyes. Her deep blue gaze met his from under shy, eager lashes. Her silver hair was still short—he had so liked it long—but it seemed as if she might be growing it out. It caressed her bronzed shoulders, calling out for his touch. He obeyed, pulling strands through his fingers.

My wife. I have a wife....

The thought stopped him, made him blink. If he didn't already know her magic, he would have been certain that he'd been enchanted. Another month had passed since he'd decided to send her on her way, yet ten minutes in her presence had reduced him to mush.

He dropped his hand. "You have to go," he said. "Take the orchid. I've included instructions on how to re-seed it."

Her cloak slipped off her elbows, whooshing to the floor,

leaving her in a thin sheath of a dress. "But what about our partnership? And my payment? I am so very thankful, you know."

The poisoner stepped away. It took all he had. "You never
wanted me before now. You don't think I know what you're
doing?"

She didn't draw closer, but it felt like she had. With a
fingertip, she traced a circle on the pale wood planks of the
counter. Leaning to the side enough for her neckline to shift.

Shoulders askew, she said, "Clever, clever. You caught me.
I'm here to beat you at your very own game." She bent forward,
and the dress fell loose enough to show everything. If he got
any harder, his penis might snap.

"Please go," he said.

"Oh," she said, "I will."

And then she struck, weaving her vertigo, her dragon magic
warping the air. When he came back to himself, he was naked,
one arm slung over the counter to keep himself up. The woman
knelt at his feet, her dress down to her waist—

And he was ejaculating onto her face.

Through the haze and the pleasure, he could only experience it. The white liquid spurted to the left of her nose as she
moved her head back to take him to her lips. He made a helpless sound as her mouth opened, her tongue pulling him in. As
she swallowed the last of his spasms.

When he was soft, she released him. "Have I pleased you,
milord?" she asked.

The word sent shivers through him, the power of it. "Yes,"
he replied, his voice ragged, though their lovemaking seemed
out of a dream. He could remember none of its details, only the
feel of it.

Sumi. You forgot Sumi....

The woman took his spare hand and lifted it to the cum on

her cheek, using his fingers to draw it to her mouth. She licked it off her lips as if the taste enthralled her.

"Milord, do you want more?"

He couldn't breathe from the want, couldn't think from the guilt. He'd told her no. How had this happened?

She placed her hands on his bare hips. "My magic skips things, Master Form. But those things would have happened, whether I used my magic or not. And so you see, it is useless to deny me.

"Now, shall I skip again, so you can have more?"

He nodded before he could even consider it. She was right, of course. He'd never stood a chance. The moment she walked through his door, Sumi became nothing.

She skipped time, and he was inside her.

He lay on his back, sprawled across his own counter. He'd conceived a child on this very spot, once. Now he clutched at the wood, his erection back up to snuff, as the woman rocked him to the rhythm of dreams. He'd masturbated to this image so many times, and now it was happening, and he was insensate.

"I forgot how long you were, milord," she moaned to him. "I forgot how good you feel."

He gripped her forearms, her hands pressed to his chest, both hands just barely pinching his nipples. "Tell me I feel better than he does."

For a moment, the woman stopped.

As her wet muscle went still on her ride down his shaft, the poisoner knew he'd crossed a line. But they were the same lines that she had been crossing. If she could take Sumi, then he—

Her hand shot to his throat. The world blinked and rolled. Skip after skip after skip. Each time he recovered, she rocked him, and fought off his next attempt to get free. Soon his vision was black and his breath was gone, and still she rode him onto the brink.

At the last second, the last moment, where he knew that he'd die, she let go. The world skipped, and they were thrusting again.

She didn't say anything, her head thrown back to take him, her legs spreading and closing with every push. His head fell back; he'd gotten the message. *Do that again, and you die, in the way you deserve.*

He would never do it again.

While he struggled to get all his oxygen back, she cried out his name, his real name. He felt her come against him; she hadn't faked it. But she didn't slow.

The black spots receded from his vision, his gasping sated his lungs. His nearness to death made his balls quiver. He watched her fey hair whip about, her breasts swinging together, nipples pointing in every direction.

"Milord!" she shrieked. "Milord!"

His orgasm came like a lull, making him smile dumbly, his body trying to go limp as it jerked. And in that moment, he knew that this fantasy was a lie—that every word she spoke was a lie. He was not her lord; he never would be. If anyone was a vassal, it was him.

When she climbed off, she said, "So that's what I've been missing." He knew she didn't mean it.

But he'd play the game. Live in the fantasy. He'd do it until it killed him—and the poisoner knew that it would. He had always known.

The woman shifted her stance, looking down at his orchid. She flicked at its petals. "Just one?"

"Just one," he agreed, and she plucked a black petal, and placed his greatest poison on the tip of her tongue.

ELEVEN

THE MAGELORD'S WHORE

TRIGGERS: MF, MOURNING, (CONSENSUAL) RAPE FANTASY, BDSM, AGE DIFFERENCE, EMPLOYER/EMPLOYEE. COMPANION BOOK: FIRST OF HER KIND. SPOILERS: SLIGHT.

REMNIS

Lord Remnis Scan shivered as he watched the sulphuric pool bubble, gripping a chunk of bluegold the size of an eye. He turned the twisted ore in his hands, the dawn light tracing every shining dip and curve. The whole thing looked like blue copper, brilliant and raw. Dragons loved it.

And so had his wife.

His chest seized at the thought of Fire, and before he could reconsider, he threw the ore at his overseer, Jerim. The man startled and nearly dropped the priceless thing.

"Milord—"

"I need you to plant that in the river today."

"Milord?"

Remnis pulled back a shoulder to look at the handsome young man. "The most beautiful woman in camp. The one they all talk about. I don't know her name."

Jerim's eyes darted, as if he were in trouble. "Do you mean Hinoda?" he asked.

Hinoda. I will have to remember that.

"If she's the one that comes to mind, yes," Remnis replied. He hadn't had anyone particular in mind. Just a woman with beauty and stories told about her. That's what drew the dragons.

A second thought struck him. "You don't fancy her, do you?" he asked Jerim. He didn't need another man's jealousy to deal with on top of everything else.

"Well—no, milord. But we may have... well—"

"Slept together?"

Jerim gulped.

Remnis huffed a short laugh. "It's all right, man. As long as you don't fancy her." He dipped his head at the ore again. "Plant that in her area today. When she finds it, send her to the manor, as normal." Any really good finds were sent back in that same fashion, but Remnis wanted to ensure this would happen.

He waved a hand. "Go, then."

Jerim went.

The sun rose higher, drawing pink lines on the water. Remnis felt the time pass in every whisper of wind.

Fire. Fire used to sit here.

It had not been her name, but it's what he had called her. A woman who gave off warmth, whose hair shone like embers, who could burn any obstacle in her path—or in his. Without her, he'd never have become magelord of Doraegon. He'd never have become a mage at all.

The sulphuric pool before him was warm, but he sat a little apart from it, on the stone bench where his wife used to read.

The mist wafted off the water in twining ribbons, always like two figures dancing. He felt its heat, but at the same time he didn't.

"I'm sorry, my darling," he said.

His wife did not answer. She'd been dead for too long. But he imagined her smile in every twinkle off the water. She would have wanted him to move on—he knew this—but Remnis himself had never desired it. And so here he sat, justifying his actions to a spirit who had already forgiven him.

"It's just that... Eidan is returning home. For the Tribute." It only occurred once every seven years, and his wife had died shortly after the last one. "I cannot allow the dragons to choose him as their sacrifice. And so I cannot allow him to be lured by love, or by legends. If I take away the most beautiful woman...."

He trailed off, ashamed. *Take away. As if she were property.* Now *that* would have made his wife angry.

But it's what dragons loved to eat: people with stories, people with love. Legendary lovers, typically of the romantic kind, although once before, he'd seen a mother and child taken.

"I can't allow him to fall in love while he is here. I'll be sending the women away every day, for early panning. I'll pay them bonuses," he added quickly, as if that made it all better. It was torture to pan for bluegold in this weather.

But... my son, he thought.

He stood up, so suddenly he even caught himself by surprise; he nearly toppled as he put too much weight on his maimed foot, half of which he'd lost to frostbite seven years ago. "I'll keep him safe. I promise you."

It was all he could do for Fire now.

Turning away from the pool with its shimmering rainbow of colors—blues and greens, but also oranges, yellows—he faced the bare forest and limped away without looking back. In seven years he had only ever returned to this place to hide his spare bluegold in the water, under a stone, where he imagined it might comfort his wife's spirit. Returning in this fashion—to speak to her, and to truly *look* at the place—well, it hurt just as much as he'd expected it to hurt. So it was with relief that he entered the forest, following a well-worn but hidden path. He suspected Eidan visited this place every time he came home, or else the path would have grown over by now.

When he glimpsed the first apple tree, he truly felt the cold. He hadn't worn a coat, although it was still the tail end of winter. He'd wanted to feel sharp, alive, but he only felt numb as he passed through the apple trees and onto the mountain path.

Where he nearly collided with a beautiful woman.

"Goat tits!" she cried, at the same time he said, "Excuse me."

They stared at each other. Her delicate hand rose to her mouth, realizing what she'd said, and whom she had said it to. He knew it was Hinoda instantly, already being sent to his manor from her false discovery. He hadn't expected to meet her so soon, nor for her to be quite this beautiful. Ebony of skin and eye, and even of *hair*. Usually, Grynn women had white or silver locks, but hers were as black and coiled as the sky between stars.

In comparison to her—even much cleaner and better-dressed—he must look a monster, with his crippled foot and scarred nose.

She fell to one knee abruptly, bowing her head like a man. "My Lord Remnis," she exhaled. "I'm terribly sorry. You startled me."

"I have a habit of startling people," he said gruffly.

"Please, I beg your forgiveness."

Dragons above, did he sound angry? He supposed he always sounded angry.

"Why are you not up the mountain?" he said. Yes, he definitely sounded angry.

She quivered, and he hated himself, but he was too paralyzed and too out of habit to make an apology. He was about to condemn this poor woman to a living hell. If he began apologizing now, he'd never go through with it.

"I—I found a large deposit of bluegold this morning, milord," she said, fumbling about in her threadbare coat. Was that truly *all* she'd been wearing up there, in this cold? "I was to visit you and give you this." She held out the same bluegold chunk he had handed off to Jerim an hour past.

Jerim had proven trustworthy yet again. It always somewhat surprised Remnis. He didn't take the bluegold.

"Have you nothing better to wear?" he said.

He meant to keep warm, something *warmer* to wear, but of course it came out all wrong. She looked up at him with wild fear. She would not have a *better* coat; she was an indenture, *his* indenture. She probably had little money of her own.

"My-my-my lord...." Her teeth were chattering. Gods, he was horrible.

He fished inside a pocket and procured a coin, fresh out of the new Corinth mint. He flipped it at her. "Procure something warmer, and then come to my manor. You can deliver the bluegold then."

He thought about saying something more, about softening the fear that must already be raging through her—but he let her feel it instead. If she believed he might take her without her consent, then when he inevitably did *not*, whatever he *did* do would seem less awful by contrast.

"See you don't delay," he said sourly, and with that, he left her alone on the trail.

HINODA

Hinoda already had a very nice coat. A gift from Jerim, which he'd used to seduce her last year. She never dared wear it panning. She wouldn't want to ruin the lace.

And so Hinoda was left with a fat coin and nothing to spend it on as she watched Remnis stagger into the forest.

And stagger he did, every movement a limp. She even thought she heard him curse when his form stumbled out of sight. Why did the foolish man not use a cane? He must have something to prove.

He's Remnis Scan. He doesn't need a cane. He doesn't need anything whatsoever. But he does want things.

And I am one of them.

Hinoda was familiar with how men like Remnis worked. She was familiar with her own good looks. Winks and crude whispers followed her wherever she went. She'd kept a knife on her at all times since age twelve.

But a knife would be useless against a magelord. Even if his magic had something to do with farming—she had never been entirely clear on what abilities their liege dragon had bestowed on him—he was the lord of an entire *region*. Killing him would earn her a death sentence from the other lords, if not from her own fellow indentures. Such rebellion could not be tolerated nor condoned. His rule kept the region stable, and without him, there would be blood.

Therefore, if he wanted her, he had the power to force her. The thought terrified her. But it also excited her.

Shut up, she told her own thoughts, but they refused. The fantasy lit her up from the inside. Oh, she knew that such an experience would be hideous—yet the thought of it still enticed her, in a pleasant, aching way. Her fantasies often centered around mystery men sneaking into her room at night, covering her mouth, and having their way with her. She'd tried to enact this with another lover once, but it had only annoyed the man. He was one of the ones who liked to use his tongue first.

Still, however morbidly excited she was at this very sick prospect, this was *Remnis* she was talking about. He must be more than two decades her senior... and that odious scar... and that *limp*.

Speaking of the limp... *I could probably overpower him if he tried something,* she told herself, finally standing to head down the path. The man could barely walk straight with only half a foot left. At the very least, she could outrun him.

But he was powerful in other ways. *Very* powerful. Aside from dragons, there were only four richer men in all the new kingdoms. Remnis owned her indenture, and the indentures of dozens of others. One could say that Remnis owned *her*.

Heart picking up pace, she practically skidded down the shale gravel at the bottom of the path, and raced for the shack she shared with her friend, Kori. Inside, she hastily bathed with a washtub of frigid water, perfumed herself (another gift from a paramour), and thrust on the lace coat.

And by the time she was presentable, she'd decided what to do with the coin.

REMNIS

"A cane," Remnis said bluntly.

Hinoda flinched at his tone. "Yes, milord," she said, holding out her "gift" to him in both palms. She was kneeling again, this time in front of his desk. She presented the cane the same way a swordsmith might present a blade.

"I don't need a cane," he replied, though it came out as a snarl. He curled his lip at the sight of the thing, as tall as his leg and made of burnished cherry wood that had been carved with bold, arced lines. Parts had been burned black and then lacquered. It reminded him of a diving falcon. He hated that he almost liked it.

Hinoda pulled back the gift, her grip uncertain as she cradled it against her chest. Her breasts were more obvious— and more ample—now that she wore nicer clothing. But her hair was ratty, the curls frizzing in all directions. Typical of an indenture, but not of a lady. A small white flower, a winterbud, had even gotten stuck on the top of her head. It must have caught there on her trip to the manor.

Her eyelashes fluttered as she dared to meet his eye. "I just thought—"

"You thought wrong," he snapped. She winced. Her breaths came in short bursts, and he became aware—too suddenly—of her position before him, on her knees. The last woman to kneel so had been Fire—

And he didn't want to think of Hinoda like that.

Growling to himself, he snatched the cane from her grip. She actually resisted a moment before letting it go, as if he were seizing a child from her; and he slammed it onto his apple wood desk with a careless thunk.

"Where is the bluegold?" he huffed. Might as well get this pretense out of the way.

She frowned, eyes landing on the cane again. "It's on the end. See?" She pointed to the curved top end of the cane, where a loop of wood enclosed the bluegold chunk; he could only see it from one side. "Originally it had a piece of quartz," she explained, "but I had the carver alter it so—"

"Idiot," he said, before clenching his mouth closed. As he beheld the cradled bluegold—which, he had to admit, looked very regal—he wondered when he'd gotten so quick to insult, to terrify. Fire would have slapped him for this.

"You're angry," Hinoda said, breathily. The tone caught him by surprise, and when he looked back at her, his eyes widened as desire flashed through her gaze. As if—as if she *wanted* him angry.

But then it was gone. He must have imagined it.

He sighed. Was he going mad?

Unable to stomach any more of his own cruel foibles, he yanked open a drawer on the desk and snatched a bracelet out of it. He tried to pretend the piece of jewelry meant nothing to him as he casually dropped it at Hinoda's knees.

"You're pretty enough," he said, as if this meant nothing, too. "I have a proposition for you. Be my wife."

Silence as she took this in. Then, "My lord...."

"I will give you Immunity from the Tribute," he said, still staring across the barren room of half-empty bookshelves and uninteresting portraits, taking care not to look anywhere near her. "I earned it for my late wife, but it passes on to any future wives I obtain. So you cannot be taken as a sacrifice to a dragon as long as you are mine."

Her mouth opened. Stayed open. Then, "That is... incredibly generous—"

"Of course it is," he shot back, annoyed. Everyone alive feared the dragons, and Immunity was the only way to stay safe from them. Not that it had helped Fire.

"In addition, you will live in the mansion," he added, "and treated like a lady. Your indenture will be considered paid. It's a good deal," he added, finally turning back to stare past her head. Even in his peripherals, he could tell she looked stunned, her eyes and mouth both wide open. This last drew his gaze to her mouth, to her plump lips. For less than an instant, he understood that those lips would touch him, if she accepted. That they might touch him *anywhere.*

He glimpsed her chest rising in a slow, labored breath, and imagined trapping his penis between them.

Oh, gods. He couldn't think of this. It had been too long, and Fire... how could he *not* think of Fire? How could he allow another woman into his bed?

"But you—you already have an heir," Hinoda finally managed to say.

He exhaled. Marriage in this region was only binding when the woman in the relationship became pregnant.

"I don't need another heir," he assured her. "I just need a woman who appears to be trying." *And I just need you away from Eidan. Far away.*

"But then why...?"

"I tire of this. Either answer, or don't."

Another pause. He felt her presence the same way he might feel the presence of a campfire, burning right there on the floor of his office.

Then he jumped—she had touched him. Her hand on his knee.

"Do you want me... to start now?" she said.

Something caught in his throat. She was saying yes. He was going to be married. He was going to have sex again. With her.

It was too much. His mind reeled. A part of him hadn't believed this would really happen.

"I am too busy," he said, a lie. He was incredibly nervous instead, so much so that his penis was still only half-hardened at her insinuation. "Tonight, I will come to you."

"When?"

"When I please."

Her breath was coming short again, and once more he faced her. Her cheeks had flushed, a button had come loose on her bodice. She looked *young*, small and firm and full of energy. He wouldn't last a second beneath her.

"Yes, milord." She rose. "I—I would be honored to be your wife...."

She trailed off, and he knew the truth. She would be *honored* to have Immunity and wealth, not him. But those things were worth nothing compared to his son, and he'd gladly give them all to her to protect Eidan from the dragons.

Hinoda turned to go, another surprising mistake. "Did I say you could leave?" he growled.

She stopped, hugged her arms. She seemed so small, and nothing like Fire. He nearly ended it right then. She deserved a future with a man who could love her.

Nonsense. Being a magelord's wife is *a future.*

Remnis rang the bell for a servant to escort her. "You may go now," he said.

"I'm sorry about the cane," she blurted. "I just... heard you stumbling in the woods today...."

He scowled at her, then back to the cane's finely made capstone. Damn whatever indentured artisan had carved it so meticulously, and damn this woman for spending her own money on the thing. Now he would *have* to use it.

He waved her forward with only his fingers. She returned to him, her neck flushing with color.

Then he reached up, and her breath caught as he plucked the winterbud out of her hair.

She stared at it in horror. "Milord, I did wash—"

"Of course you washed," he sighed. "This is a winterbud. Very rare. They fall from weeping birches at the end of winter. My late wife adored them."

She fell quiet. So did he. He realized that the cruelty had gone out of his tone.

He didn't like it. "Get out."

⊕

HINODA

Under the coat, Hinoda had worn her best dress, a flowing violet wrap with a beaded bodice. Another gift from a suitor, which suddenly seemed so shabby compared to the other dresses hanging in the closet of the room she'd been given. Afraid to leave her new apartments, she spent the last half of the day exploring what must have been the late Lady Scan's clothing. Luscious emerald velvet, sultry red silk, mountains of lace dyed in shades of blue dawn. She had always enjoyed the finer things herself, but Lady Scan had a keen eye for detail. Hinoda might have tried the things on, if she'd thought they would fit.

As it was, she had too much in the chest area... and the hip area... and basically all areas. She had almost never seen the Lady Scan, but where Remnis was moderately large and entirely imposing, the Lady had been diminutive. But also, somehow, still imposing.

Hinoda was not imposing. Hinoda was not anything. She was beautiful, perhaps, and she had a decent sense of humor. But she wasn't a lady. She was more like a harlot.

This fact had never embarrassed her before. But in front of these dresses, she felt differently.

She spent the last hours of daylight pacing her rooms and picking at the tray of biscuits a servant had brought her. When darkness fell, she set about lighting candles and scented oils and setting an atmosphere however she could. If she was to be a lord's wife, and to have Immunity, then she needed to put forth more effort than simply lying on her back. Surely.

Another hour passed. Still he did not come.

It was the cane. A hare-brained scheme if she'd ever had

one. She had tried to convince herself she intended it as a thoughtful overture, but in truth, she had known it might anger him. That anger had led to desire, pooling low in her stomach as she knelt before him.

She must be mad, to kick the wolf in such a way. A deliciously powerful wolf....

Another hour passed. She grew tired. Soon her fear and misplaced lust were replaced by exhaustion. She fought to keep her eyes open, and failed. She slept.

When she woke, the fire in her hearth had died down low, casting the elegant curtains and wood paneling in a soft orange glow. Part of a moon cut through the corner of one window.

Immediately, she felt his presence.

Instantly, her body woke, but the rest of her did not. She had fantasized over something like this so often that she reacted with precision: even breathing, stillness, slitted eyes as she scanned her surroundings.

He sat before the fireplace, in one of two armchairs. In one hand he held a glass tumbler—liquor, perhaps? In his other, he gripped the cane. He was still. Watching her.

No—not watching her. She moaned softly, a sleep-noise, and shifted to get a better look at him. He wasn't looking at her, but past her. Though his scarred face was in shadows, there was no menace about him.

Then he sighed, a resigned noise, nothing like the hunger she expected. She forgot to feign sleep as he knocked back the rest of the liquor and slammed it loudly on a glass-topped side table. Hinoda sat up sharply, drawing a hard breath, leaning on her arms.

"Ah, so you're awake, then," he said gruffly, pulling an object from his coat pocket and tossing it at her. It landed beside her left hand. A hairbrush—a very fine hairbrush. White horsehair. She'd never seen one of such quality before, its handle carved from some kind of bone and emblazoned with winterbuds.

"I'm told it works better than a comb," he said, standing up, and drawing closer with the thunk of his cane. The bed had four posts and a canopy, and he snared one post with his spare arm, leaning into it.

"It... does work better. Much better," she replied. "I... I haven't seen one since I was a girl."

"Ah."

Silence.

He cleared his throat. "So you're saying all the women in my camp have hair as unruly as yours?"

Hinoda smiled. "And some of the men."

Remnis sniffed, a laugh perhaps. More silence. He *loomed*, and the shadow he cast upon her felt like a blanket drawing back. She pulled her legs in and looked up at him. One sleeve of her dress shifted to reveal a bare shoulder.

Desire flooded her as his eyes met flesh. In that moment, he was not older than her, or crippled, or scarred. He was a hulking shape in the darkness. A dangerous shape, full of wanting.

Her pulse was a storm as she placed the hairbrush on the bedside table and rose from the bed. Despite the time of day, she'd never felt more awake as she stepped nearer to him, circling around to his back. He tilted his head to keep his eyes on her, though his body remained still, facing forward.

When she was close enough to kiss him, she leaned against his back. He still watched her, his head turned, his gaze thrown back over his own shoulder. They were close enough that she felt his breath on her lips.

She said, "Tell me what to do, milord."

He blinked. "You're a virgin?"

She shuddered pleasantly. "No. Does that bother you?"

"No," he replied, but his tone remained gruff. "It's just— shouldn't you know what to do?"

Hinoda laid her hands on his hips and kissed the skin beneath his ear. "I like to be ordered," she whispered.

He stopped breathing, which made her ache. No man had ever had this reaction before. No man remained still while she kissed him. It was almost as if he wanted her *more,* so much more that he didn't dare touch her, for fear of losing control.

His next words were raw, the edges duller than before. "Your clothes," he said. "Take them off."

She nodded, and circled him, letting one hand trail across his lower back and around his waist to his stomach. Standing before him now, she met his eyes and reached both hands to her bodice, capturing the strings with her fingertips, and pulling.

The beaded bodice loosened, and she exhaled as her breasts sagged forward, pulling the strings ever looser. Curling her fingers into the very edge of her neckline, she tugged the fabric lower, until the deeper color of her nipples began to show through the sheer material. He tensed, his eyes locked on her breasts as she teased the bodice lower, and lower, and lower....

A dull *thunk* made her start, and she glanced down to see he'd tossed his cane aside. Then his freed hand found her waist and rose, fingers running over the beads until his thumb could tug the edge of the dress down just *enough*. Her right nipple appeared, and she inhaled to bring her breasts higher, to force the other nipple free as well. The bodice fell limp around her waist, and his hand cupped her breast, his thumb dipping into the hard point in the center.

All the time, she watched his face raptly. His gaze had been intense on her body, but now he closed his eyes and shuddered.

"Milord...."

"Touch me," he said.

Her hands fell to his belt, slipped the loops, and yanked.

He nearly fell against her, caught by surprise at her ferocity. But she was eager to feel him. To start the pleasing. And to feel a magelord finish inside her.

"Hinoda—" he choked out, but she cut him off with her hand, encircling his penis inside a hard grip. He flinched.

He was thick and hot and hard, but still he grimaced as she slid her other hand around to the back of his neck and tickled. With one hand she tickled his hair, while with the other she pumped him, just one time, getting a sense of his length.

Her chest fluttered. He would feel good. All she had to do was please him, and she would get to feel this inside her. She stroked.

He swayed against her with each movement, breathing in rasps. It reminded her of the last virgin she'd been with, who acted as if each squeeze were an unbearable surprise. His hips began to buck, his penis to sweat. Her own heat spread and wept for mercy. Beads of liquid spread under her thumb as she prodded his head, rubbing him clean again.

His grip tightened on her chest, circling her breast, exploring it. Then suddenly his other hand raced up the bedpost and he threw his head back and cursed. She thought he would come then, but he didn't, just kept rocking and breathing hard, his throat-apple bobbing in front of her eyes as she leaned closer to it, kissing his chin.

He brought his face to hers, their eyes meeting, the tip of her nose whispering over his scar. Then he dropped her breast and curved a fist into her skirts and shoved her sideways. Within seconds he'd positioned himself above her, on his hands and knees, fumbling at her skirts. The way he breathed made her tug him closer. He grunted as her hand rose into his short hair and clawed at his scalp.

He seized her wrist and shoved her hand off him before thrusting her skirts up—

And swinging inside her.

It was that fast, that forceful. She moaned, long and shuddery. His penis collided to a stop, so deep her stomach tensed. She gasped his name, not his title. *"Remnis...."*

He was shaking, dropping his head beside her chin as he pulled out and thrust again. Her legs tightened around him, her ankles locking together, her back arching to pull him straight into her. Her forehead tensed from the pleasure, her mouth open, soundless. One more time. Two more times. Three.

She'd done this before, many times, and with bigger penises too. But this time felt new, more intense. Something in the way he shook, in his age... it made him seem vulnerable. And it made her feel *wanted*, treasured even. The young lover, the object of desire.

Her hands raced down his back and pulled at his flesh, leading him into her faster. He leaned away, looking down at her chest, mouth open. He gripped her breast again with one hand, stared intently at it.

His eyes closed. He shook his head. Again she thought he was coming, but no—it was—it was the *opposite*. He was *softening*.

Remnis paused, sweating, and she remembered his injured foot. Was it causing him pain? He cursed.

"Milord—"

"Your knees," he said, rolling onto his back. He pulled on her waist and she arced over top of him, her breasts pressing hard to his chest. He was hairless there, smooth, as if he had shaved. As if he had wanted to feel her flesh on his.

"Your knees," he said again. He was gripping himself now, stroking. Trying to harden again, maybe? Confusion seared through her. What had she done wrong? Why was he soft?

She placed her hand over his. "Let me do that."

"No."

"Milord—"
"I said *get on your knees.*"
And she did.

REMNIS

Hinoda slid off the bed to her knees with a thunk, and Remnis sat up to look at her. He kept his hand going hard as her skirts billowed around her, as she leaned her face close. Hungrily.

As if she—as if she would *suck on him.*

His desperate hand slowed, and he let go. Outlined her breasts, her shoulders, then her lips with his gaze. She leaned closer. No. Would she really—

He groaned as her lips closed on his head, as her tongue licked her own fluids off him. Fire had never done this. She'd insisted they stay clean—

Fire. Oh, skies. *Fire.*

He softened again, shoulders hunching forward. He couldn't do this. Not with another woman. She was so beautiful, so *experienced,* but he couldn't—

Hinoda sucked his soft penis down *hard.*

Remnis bucked in pain, snatching at her head, sinking his fingers into her thick curls. But once there, she released him before sucking down again, and he didn't know if he wanted to shove her off or take the pain.

In the end, he was helpless. He let her work, let her slowly convince him that his late wife had never existed, that there was only Hinoda and her mouth and her frown of concentration and the subtle movements of her arm as she touched herself, thrusting a finger against her clitoris in time to her tongue.

He hardened more at that last than at anything. To think that she was enjoying this... that she wasn't the barely-willing partner he'd expected....

Just as this thought flitted through him, Hinoda's lips stopped gripping him. Her mouth opened around his penis, and he felt her breath pass hot and steamy across the rigid flesh. She panted and licked, panted and sucked and exhaled until she pressed her forehead into his stomach and twisted against his navel. Her moan was as crazed as he felt, with her one hand around him, her cheek pressed to his penis, and her other hand slowing between her legs.

Orgasm. She had just come. He hadn't even done anything, and it had happened so fast. How had she managed it? How did she *want* him?

He didn't have time to consider this before her mouth slammed down on him again. He grunted as her teeth pricked him, and he cried out a moment later as she seized his hips and forced him into her cheek, her tongue, her molars. He wanted to cry, he was so hard, harder than she should have ever been for a woman who was not... who was not....

But he couldn't hold his late wife's name in his mind any longer. The clacking sounds of Hinoda's lips and the heat of her tongue kicked every other thought from his head, until he was huffing and puffing like an old man, his need curdling in his testicles, burning and squeezing and then—

With a thrust to the back of her throat, he came, feeling the vibration of her surprised murmur in the fleshy head of his penis. Pulse after pulse, he ejaculated into her, and she began to suck again as he softened, as if to get the rest out of him.

When it was over, her dark eyes rose to his. What did she see? An exhausted old man? He felt bewildered, unreal. Fire flitted through his mind and back out again. It had been seven years since he'd come inside any part of a woman, and his breath rattled as he released it. She drew off him with a quiet *slurp,* then pulled the bedsheet to her mouth like a napkin and spat. He watched the white of his body slick the fabric.

Somehow, seeing it there—that took him back to reality. He surged to his feet, throwing her backward. She landed with an ungainly thump, her breasts bouncing. Damn those breasts.

He folded his manhood hastily back into his pants. "It's done then," he said. He wasn't even clear what he meant. Until he could come inside her, until she had a chance of being pregnant, she could not be considered his true wife, could not obtain the Immunity.

She watched his buckle as if she didn't agree that "it" was done, either. Her chest heaved like she wanted more.

This wasn't what he'd prepared for. She wasn't timid or afraid of him. She had put herself *into* this. She had acted with *desire.*

Hinoda had asked for orders, and he had given them, had forgotten the entire reason he was here to begin with. This was supposed to be a marriage of necessity, to keep his son safe. But now it seemed like the selfish machinations of an old man who craved a young lover.

His late wife's face sprang to his mind. *I'm so sorry, Fire....*

Hinoda's gaze met his own, sudden and blazing. "Tell me what to do. *Please.*"

She was still breathing hard. Still *ready.* The sheer *madness* of it floored him. Was she really asking to make him hard again? Dragons take him.

"No," he said, meaning it to sound angry. But even to his own ears, he sounded astonished. Probably because he *was.*

Disappointment sparked across her eyes, and he backed away from her, limping as he recovered his cane and used it. The support it provided was a balm to his ravaged body. Hinoda stood, still not bothering to hide her breasts. Guileless.

"When can I have you next?" she asked.

When can I have you. Not *when can you impregnate me.* It wasn't supposed to go this way. She was not supposed to *want* him.

"I'll—" his voice was dry. He straightened his shoulders. "I will... let you know."

Well *that* wasn't very forceful. How weak he must look. She rose back onto the bed, baring her chest in defiance. His groin twitched. Her breasts were so large....

She saw him looking, and ran a hand over her right nipple, twirling the darker flesh with one fingertip. "If you stay," she purred, "I can get you ready again."

Curses ravaged his brain. It was too much. He shook his head no.

Then he fled.

✹

HINODA

Her lord Remnis avoided Hinoda all the next day. A scowling servant summoned her to an empty breakfast table, where she ate from more plates than she'd ever seen in one place. Then a scowling maid dressed her in her only other dress, a simple red number with a plunging back and slitted leg. Then a scowling steward offered her a tour of her new home, including the bedroom of her new stepson, Eidan, who had arrived the night before but was currently out.

Scowling, scowling, scowling. None of them believed she deserved Remnis. All of them thought her a whore.

Well, let them think it. Let *Remnis* think it, if he wanted. She'd never been shy about enjoying sex. She just wondered if she'd ever have it again, because at the rate she was going, she'd be an old lady before she found out where her new lord was hiding. Had she really done so poorly last night? Her own mouth watered at the thought of his commands. *Touch me. I said get on your knees!*

But he'd gone soft inside her, and then he'd run from her as if terrified. She'd never once had a man do that before, especially not after offering, topless, to get them going for a second round. And so she wandered her new two-story manse, alone, hoping to cross paths with him, thinking of all the ways she could have done better. After practically memorizing the entire home, she finally worked up the courage to enter his office just as night had begun to fall. He was absent from the room, which she'd known already, but perhaps she could wait for him here. Maybe sprawl out on the desk beneath the portrait of that woman....

Her eyes lingered on the wall hanging. When she'd first seen it, she'd believed it to be fanciful artwork, as the woman pictured had flaming red hair. Such a color didn't exist, as far as she knew, and yet... why was it there, behind his desk?

She approached the image, ran her fingers over the thick ridges of paint. The woman's gaze was intense, fierce even, and what at first had seemed a relaxed pose now appeared to Hinoda to be taut and ready.

The door clicked behind her. She spun.

Remnis stood, eyes wide, on the threshold. When their gazes met, he swallowed, his eyes flicking to the painting.

Hinoda sensed he was about to flee. "Was she your wife?" she blurted.

She expected—perhaps distantly even craved—a flare of anger. Instead he sidled into the room and closed the door quietly. Still facing away from her, he said, "Yes, she was."

Hinoda's breath caught. *Pain.* She heard it so clearly in his voice.

"So that's why," she exhaled. He turned to her.

"You don't have permission to be here," he said, without inflection.

She rounded the desk and approached him. He actually backed away a step, so she paused just within arm's length of him.

"Apparently it's my house now," she said.

"You're not my wife yet."

"Not for lack of trying."

Again, she thought he'd lash out, perhaps even strike her. He instead began to stare intently at the far corner of the room.

"Leave," he said.

"Why?"

His eyes closed. He inhaled. The breath rattled.

"If you need to—with another man," he stammered, "then I'll claim the child as mine."

Hinoda flinched. "What?"

"I'll call you my wife and give you the Immunity. Even if the child isn't mine."

For a long second, Hinoda had no response to this. Finally, she huffed out, "No."

"I know you're... hungry. Experienced—"

"No," she said stoutly.

"I can't give you what—"

"You gave me plenty of what I wanted last night," she snapped. "I can be patient, you know. I don't need to fuck twenty times a day. I just thought that's what *you* wanted. What else would a lord expect?"

He hung his head. When was he going to get angry? She realized, for the first time, that he'd been using the cane she had given him. He'd carefully propped it up beside the door.

"I will not cheat on you," she declared.

"It wouldn't be—"

"Yes, milord, it *would* be cheating. And I might enjoy sex, but I will not cheat on a man I've committed to." She stepped closer, so that her chest pressed against his. He recoiled, his neck muscle tight as a bowstring as he forced himself not to peer into her cleavage. "And, milord Remnis, I have committed to you. Have you done the same for me?"

***

REMNIS

He craved her. She must be able to feel it now, that embarrassing, hateful need between his legs. All day, he'd been unable to think of anything else. Hating himself for running from her last night. Hating himself for not treasuring Fire.

He glanced at her painting now, at those blazing green eyes. Hinoda raised a hand to his face and forced his gaze away, drawing him into her dark, pitiless eyes.

"You loved her," she said. It sounded like an accusation.

He swallowed.

"I can't have been the first, Remnis," she said, and a fresh ache stuttered to life in his chest. When was the last time someone had called him by his name, with no title? "Surely you've rolled in the hay with other women since. It's been seven years, right? So what's wrong with *me?*"

His pulse filled his ears, blocking out the sounds of the early evening birds. When he'd come home, he'd asked his steward what Hinoda had done in his absence. She'd paced the house aimlessly, claiming to wait for him; she hadn't bossed around a single servant; she hadn't asked after Fire's jewelry or his own treasury or even the Immunity.

This was supposed to be a business transaction. The title of "wife" and the safety of his son, all in exchange for Immunity.

When he didn't respond, Hinoda's eyebrows rose. She leaned away. "No one?" she whispered.

He shook his head, his mouth too dry for words.

"You haven't had sex with *anyone?* In seven *years?*"

He was abruptly seized by the urge to thrust her against a wall and scoop up her skirts and just go.

"Miss Hinoda," he croaked. "I don't understand you." He *needed* to understand where his power had gone. Why he felt so helpless.

Why she wanted *him.*

Her gaze hardened, searching his face, coming to rest on his scarred nose. She stared at it with fascination, and her hand on his cheek slid over, her fingers drifting across the ridges of the ugly mark.

And then down, over his lips: Pressing one finger between them. He tasted the salt of her sweat.

Hinoda watched his mouth. "You're so powerful," she whispered. "It's hot to me." She closed her eyes, shuddered, ran a pointer finger along his tongue. "I think you believed that I was a whore. You wouldn't be the first. But the truth is, I have a fantasy, and you can provide it." She extracted her finger and rose onto her toes, bringing her lips to his. "That's why I told you yes so quickly. It's madness. I shouldn't have. But...."

She kissed him, softly, and without a conscious thought his hand came around her lower back and he pulled her against him. She released a faint gasp as his erection sank into the flesh of her thigh, with only a few layers of fabric between them.

His breath came faster. "Tell me what you want."

She didn't wait to answer. "To be taken. Roughly."

"How rough?"

She clawed at his collar. "Very."

Remnis tasted her lips, bit them. She shuddered.

"You like to be powerless?" he asked, his voice taking on a new growling inflection that even he did not recognize.

Hinoda moaned. "*Yes.*"

He tried to think, tried to see through the haze of desire. He felt so raw, inhuman. She made him think of nothing else. It couldn't last, could it? He couldn't feel this good forever. She'd tire of him, wouldn't she? Wouldn't she?

His hand at her back fisted, and he swung her around and against the wall. She bared her throat with a soft cry as he fumbled her skirts up to her waist—

A knock sounded at the door, and both of them froze.

"*What?*" Remnis snapped.

On the other side of the thick wood, his steward's voice said, "Milord, I—that is, dinner is served, as you requested."

He'd forgotten about the whole charade he'd had planned out. A dinner where he'd introduce Hinoda to his son, mostly just to make Eidan angry and to ward him off from chasing other women. When Eidan saw how he'd abused his power with Hinoda, Eidan's own self-righteousness would keep him from doing the same... at least, he'd been banking on that.

Right now, though, he wasn't hungry.

"Is my son even here?" he growled, wishing he wasn't.

"I—he didn't come through the door, milord, but I did hear noises in his room. Perhaps he entered through the window," the steward said.

Typical Eidan. Never doing anything he's told.

Remnis looked down at Hinoda. Her sumptuous breasts rose and fell against his chest, too quickly, rough from excitement. She had been watching his mouth, and now her gaze met his.

Power. She liked *power.*

Summoning every shred of self-control he had, Remnis shoved away from her and hauled open the door. "My wife will attend to dinner now," he said, snatching at her dress and yanking her into view of the steward. Her skirts barely fell back around her legs as he did so, and he pushed her through the doorway. "I'll be along shortly."

With that, he slammed the door. Silence followed.

He'd planned a show for Eidan, and it was time to perform.

HINODA

Hinoda's heart never stopped thrumming, like an overused instrument. It was all she could do to sit in her place at the table and watch Remnis eat. Fast and beastly, not looking at her. She was unimportant. She was meat.

Except for the tiny, almost imperceptible glances. His gaze asking, *Is this all right?*

It was. It *was* all right.

Remnis. Remnis. *Remnis.*

She was sweating, and it wasn't from the heat of the food. She didn't dare eat. She might throw up. The emotions running through her were so heightened that she couldn't even name them.

Without warning, Remnis stiffened. She watched his eyes dart to the ceiling, once again so quick that it would be easy to miss. She followed his gaze upward, past the bronze chandelier. There was some sort of vent just beyond it.

"Hinoda," Remnis said, his voice low and lusty. His fingers flicked at her. She understood and rose, walking toward him. Trembling.

She nearly flipped the whole table when the dining room door opened.

Her stepson, Eidan, stormed into the room. He was wide-shouldered and taller than his father, with red-tinged hair (so the color really *was* real) and colorless eyes. She found him distantly handsome, in a farmhand sort of way, but he looked brutish with the blazing rage on his face.

"Why is she wearing Mother's bracelet?" he growled at his father.

In response, Remnis snaked his hand around her, and Hinoda stiffened. His gaze rose from her neck to her toes and back up again. Ravenous. Appraising.

"It's not your mother's bracelet any longer," he said.

Eidan fumed. "You can't be serious."

"Oh, I am. This charming woman is my wife." Remnis finally met his son's eyes. "At least she will be, just as soon as she's pregnant."

A show. He was putting on a show. She was a prop. He was using her.

Yes.

Eidan's hands slammed down on the table. "What about *Mother?*"

Hinoda expected Remnis to flinch, to falter. Instead, he said coldly, "She's dead, son."

Hinoda thought she might shatter right there.

"Not to me," Eidan shot back. "And not to you, either. What is this really about?"

"It's not about anything," Remnis said, reaching for a leg of pheasant on the plate in front of him. "A man gets lonely in these mountains, is all—"

"So you take some poor girl off the farm and force her?" Eidan said. Remnis leaned forward to speak, but Eidan swept a hand at Hinoda. "Look at her, Father. She's a complete stranger. No offense, Miss Hinoda, you are very pretty, but—"

"Enough!" Remnis roared, squeezing Hinoda to his side. The movement made Hinoda realize she wasn't helping him, wasn't doing a single thing. So she twisted away, as if she really believed he might hurt her. The movement helped her lose herself in the fantasy, to the point she couldn't wait for Eidan to leave.

"Now *sit,* my son. Eat." Remnis took a bite of the pheasant. Now *he* was the brutish one. *Yes.* "Get to know your new step-mother," he went on as he chewed. *Crude.* "If we're lucky, she'll supply a new heir for the title, and you won't have to dirty your hands—"

"I've lost my appetite," Eidan snapped, drawing his hands back. He opened the door and slammed it as he left.

"Leave us," Remnis said, and the servants—Hinoda had forgotten they were there—vacated the room, as rapid as ghosts. Hinoda stifled a cry as Remnis stood and turned toward her.

"You know what I want, my dearest," he said.

Hinoda's heart hammered. "N-now?" she stammered. *Say yes.*

"Now. Or do you not want that Immunity? You'll have to be showing by the time the seekers come, or they won't see you as my wife."

Shakily Hinoda straightened. With careful hands she pushed Remnis's plate and silverware toward the center of the table, clearing enough space for her to bend over the surface. Remnis kept his hands on her hips as she reached down and lifted the hem of her dress. She heard his breath stop as her bare bottom slid into view. She'd taken the liberty of removing her undergarments. Anything to get him inside her faster.

He rubbed her butt, rolling the flesh under his calloused palms. She quivered, needing him, afraid of him. One of his hands ventured away, toward his groin, and her arms nearly gave out from the anticipation as he gathered himself in his hand.

And then his penis was touching her. Parting her lips, circling. Waiting to strike.

"My little whore," he growled.

Yes.

"My dirty little indenture, who thinks she's good enough to be my wife...."

She dropped her head, struggling not to buck against him. In a pitiful voice, she begged for mercy. "Milord, please...."

He thrust inside her so hard that every piece of silverware skittered forward. She shouted from the pressure, the raw, hard-edged pain of it. She hadn't been wet enough, not deep enough.

Y-Y-Yes....

Remnis leaned over her back and tugged her hair over one shoulder. In a bare whisper, he said, "Does this work?"

She nodded, fast, eyes winched closed. When he pulled out of her, he pulled a ragged sound from her throat.

"Do you want me to fuck you?" he growled.

Hinoda shook her head no, no no no no. But the word that she whispered was *yes.*

He slammed her into the table. She cried out, scrabbling to stay upright. He seized her hair and smacked her head into the table, hard enough to hurt but not hard enough to hurt *much.* Hinoda felt tears spring to the corners of her eyes, tears of need so intense that they fed into the fantasy perfectly. She sobbed and he pounded into her again, sliding faster now as her vagina went slick. He grunted with each push into her body, and for the first time she felt the true force of him, crippled foot and all.

"You don't like that, do you?" he said, his hip bones ramming her butt cheeks, his balls whipping past her thighs. The table inched forward once, twice, three times with his rhythm. "Beg me to stop, wife. Beg me for it, and I might relent."

"Please." The word was broken. "Please stop, *please—*"

He lifted her head and shoved it down again. She cried out. The table struck the far wall, he'd pushed it so far.

"Not good enough," he ground out, practically tearing her hair out as he yanked her back. He ran his nose along her neck, and she swallowed with perfect false terror. He nosed her ear lobe.

She sobbed again. "Please...."

He offered no gentleness as he dipped out of her and forced her to flip onto her back. Somewhere a plate fell to the ground and shattered as he spread her legs.

He entered her. She screamed. Then he thrust again, and again and again, so rapidly she couldn't shout in time to each thrust and could only cry out when she had the breath. She'd thought him old, perhaps infirm, but that wasn't the man inside her right now. He fucked with precision that didn't sacrifice speed, and the way his shaft felt inside her was like nothing she'd ever experienced. The sheer *focus* of him, a man who'd only used his own hand in seven years—*how?* How could he *do* this?

"Milord," she wept. "Oh, dragons, Remnis...."

"*Hinoda,*" he replied, the word desperate, and in those seconds the veil fell away. He slowed and slipped out of her, then kneed his way onto the table and hovered over her, his wet penis rubbing the inside of her thigh as their eyes met, as his sweat ran down his face.

She expected, *wanted* him to sink into her, but instead he watched her just long enough for her sex to feel the cold of the air.

"Will you get tired of me, Hinoda?" he said softly.

The words broke her heart instantly. She reached for the back of his neck with one hand, palmed his shoulder blade with the other. She pulled his forehead to hers.

"I've never wanted someone more in my life," she whispered as their noses touched.

He put his weight on his forearm, then used his freed hand to pull the front of her dress aside. One breast rolled out to meet him, her nipple crinkled into a point. He rubbed a thumb over it, then let go to grip her thigh. He thrust carefully into her. They both drew breath.

Remnis hung there, and though a part of her still wanted the fantasy, the rest of her mind said, *There will be time.* She didn't think she'd ever tire of him, not when he could give her this, and look at her like *this,* and not when he felt like no penis she'd ever had, like it was made to fit the inside of her body.

He dropped his head beside hers, rounded her thigh with his hand, and then fingered her clitoris. She gave a skittering moan as he moved into her, as the sensations tripled and tightened. She could feel the fleshy edges of his head popping into her and back out, swaying past the bumps and muscle inside her, making promises that came each moment closer to fruition.

"Shit," he said, his voice muffled against her ear. She waited to feel the pulse of his coming, but his finger only moved faster. As he thrust, he kept saying it. "Shit—shit—shit—"

He was holding back with all his might. Again her heart broke for him. She melted against his body, closed her legs on his hips and felt his finger and his penis and his muscular weight, right there on the kitchen table for the whole world to see.

It was coming. It was there. She gripped his tensing butt and hauled him into her, arcing her back, practically pulling his skin apart as she forced him forward faster, faster, *faster.*

Her orgasm met the rush of his thrusts, like a dammed river bursting past rock. She couldn't even speak as she clutched him, her body coiling around his. He groaned her name and jumped out of her, without warning. His hot ejaculate squirted against her inner thighs, hitting her with actual force, coming out faster than she'd ever felt before.

They breathed fast and rampant, the sweat of her chest sinking into his shirt and his sweat dripping off his head into her hair as they looked at each other. Like this, his scar made him look vulnerable. She wanted to pull him to her chest, but she just twirled a finger in his hair.

"I'll never get pregnant if you do it that way," she said. He had only just now stopped spurting.

He shook his head at her and rasped, "I want you to myself a little longer. Before we take chances."

Her chest expanded with feeling. Somehow, she was madly in love with this man whom she had never even spoken to before yesterday. It was lust, but it was also more. Something that could *become* more.

Remnis laughed abruptly. It sounded partly like a groan. "Dragons above! I'm too old for this."

She traced a finger down his jawline. "You have a whore, Remnis," she whispered. "A pathetic and weak little whore. You can make her do all the work."

Remnis chuckled again and kissed her easily. It caught her by surprise.

"I think I'd like that," he said, rolling over. More dishes broke, and his arm swung wide, to the vase of flowers she'd barely noticed. He procured a winterbud from it, then tucked it into her hair.

"Then again," he said lowly, "I also want to know what my whore tastes like. Do you think she could spread her legs, and let me find out?"

Don't miss *The Rose Contract*, Book 1 of the Sleeping Lotus series!

Please support the author by **leaving a review!**

You can also get Scottie's newsletter for updates on her new releases!

ACKNOWLEDGMENTS

To my Patreon supporters Sandra, Daniel, and Willie: you make all the difference. Thank you.

ABOUT THE AUTHOR

Scottie Kaye grew up in small-town Michigan. She smokes cigars, brews beer, and unabashedly hugs trees while also killing "unkillable" plants. She lives in the Midwest with her husband and too many cats, and is always cooking up a new story. Connect with her through the avenues below:

f g a BB

Made in the USA
Middletown, DE
06 September 2025